SWEET LOVE

LADY DEE

PROLOGUE

"Oh my gosh. Babe, you feel so good." The vibration from his deep voice tickled my earlobe, forcing my muscles to relax and loosen. The passion felt between us as our bodies intertwine goes beyond words that can be described.

I gazed into his brown eyes, beads of sweat formed across his forehead, ran down his mocha skin, and dripped onto my breasts. His stroking shortened and intensified. I spread my legs wider, digging my fingernails into the contours of his back, gently biting on my bottom lip. I moaned in pleasure taking the pressure of all one hundred and ninety pounds of muscle. His breathing heightened, I felt myself reaching climax, struggling to control the urge. I wanted the ache. I wanted him all in me, all the time.

"Oh, yes right there…," I moaned. I couldn't hold back any longer. My legs shook as he drove himself deeper.

Within seconds, my cream oozed down his strong rod and onto the silk sheets. Chris clenched his buttocks, with his legs squeezed together, giving me one last pump, before his body went limp. We breathed heavily after three hours of making love. Chris rolled onto his back and pulled me closer to him. Under the trance of the sensual music playing in the background, I lay on his chest, my mind drifting to another place.

"Babe, you really don't know what you do to me. I know you don't believe me when I tell you all I want is you, but I will prove everything in due time." Chris spoke with much emphasis and sincerity, but he was right. I didn't believe a word that was coming out of his mouth.

If only he could see me roll my eyes in the dark. I'm sure my reaction would confirm his doubts. Chris continuously tries to make the blow of him leaving me not feel so bad, but some things never change. This was a line heard all too often from Chris. I closed my eyes, holding back the tears I knew would form if he continued to speak.

"Just be patient with me, Babe. Please be patient with me." Chris pleas fell on deaf ears.

I rolled off his chest and lay on my back, staring at the ceiling in deep thought. I knew Chris loved me but I loved myself more. I was so wrapped up in my thoughts that I didn't mind the tear escaping my eye, and rolling down my cheek onto the pillowcase. Why do I keep playing myself? I deserve better, so I need to start acting like it!

Chris sensed my discomfort and reached for my hand, that I quickly snatched away from his touch. Instead of trying to grab my hand again, his head slowly went under the sheets. The sensation of the soft silk sheets against my skin relaxed me, as well as the warm wet kisses he tenderly planted on my inner thighs. As much as I wanted him to stop, I couldn't control the chills his body sent up my spine or the light puddle that formed at the center of my thighs. His touch spoke a language to my body, unlocking each area. I leaked uncontrollably. I felt the heat from his mouth as his tongue traveled to my G-spot.

Chaka Khan's voice resonated through the bedroom speakers. The words she sang in the song, "My Funny Valentine," touched my heart in more ways than one. Chris is far from perfect, but I love him despite everything. I closed my eyes and thought, *Lord, why can't I stop?*

A NEW DAY

"DON'T LOOK BACK, FOR WHAT IS DONE CANNOT BE UNDONE."

*T*he sunlight peeking through my bedroom window forced my sleepy eyes to open. I was hesitant, but I reached for my vibrating cell phone on the dresser. Just the thought of getting out of the bed after last night's festivities drained my mind. The scent of Chris's cologne lingered on the sheets, attached to my skin and left my body yearning for more. I shook my head, thinking, *I need to get myself together and stop stressing over this man.*

I ran my fingers through my tangled hair, contemplating my next move. I fought with the tangled sheets between my legs before eventually rolling over to check my cell phone. Three missed calls and six text messages were the reason my phone was vibrating off the hook. I was even more surprised when I looked at the time on the phone screen that read 11:00 a.m. *Damn! I can't believe I slept in this long on a Saturday morning!*

As much as I wanted to lie in bed, my conscience reminded me of my agenda for the day. I walked into the bathroom and looked at my naked body; perky breasts, washboard abs, and a nice, firm, round bottom. This is how I would physically describe myself, but how could such a beautiful woman have so many insecurities? As I reflected on my enormous house, flashy car, and peaceful life, I still feel incomplete. I turned to the side and poked my belly out. I did this often, hoping one day, I would have a family with a loving husband. Unfortunately, the older I got, this idea seemed more like a dream than reality.

I grabbed my toothbrush and toothpaste, pinned up my thick curly hair, making a mental note to contact my stylist this week. Taking a fresh shower with a not so fresh mouth just wasn't normal to me, or for me. I adjusted the shower water temperature and watched the steam fill the bathroom, creating a mist on the large bathroom mirror. My reflection in the mirror now revealed a silhouette of my body. I stepped into the shower, inhaling the steam in hopes that the heat would somehow wash away my sins. I closed my eyes and imagined Chris kissing the back of my neck and massaging my shoulders under the water. I loved leaning onto his chest while he caressed me under the water. There was something within him that held me captive. The tears rolling down my cheeks forced me to open my eyes. My guilt, pleasure, and pain were an ongoing battle, at times, I didn't know whether I would win or lose. *One day I will let him go, I have the strength to do it.* I whispered words of affirmation, believing one day it would be true.

Finishing up in the shower, I prepared myself for my day ahead. My bedroom looked like a tornado had gone through it, with lingerie in different corners of the room, ruffled mattress sheets, and pillows on the bedroom floor. I placed my hands on my hips, looking around at the mess and started picking up items, one by one. I stepped onto something squishy, looked down, and noticed the used condom. I picked it up and threw it in the trashcan. I was in disgust all over again. As I dwelled on my thoughts, while rinsing my hands off after touching the condom, my phone vibrated again. I rushed to grab the phone off the dresser, and almost tripped over one of my stilettos on the floor. I answered the phone just in time, without looking at the caller ID, only to hear Kesha's big mouth on the other end.

"WHY DON'T YOU ANSWER YOUR PHONE WHEN PEOPLE ARE CALLING YOU? YOU ALWAYS PUT YOUR PHONE ON VIBRATE AT NIGHT! WHAT IF THERE IS AN EMERGENCY?" Kesha yelled.

"First off, if you keep yelling, you will hear the dial tone. Secondly, I do sleep at night and I think I deserve that. Third, if it was truly an emergency, you have my spare key, Kesha, so stop over exaggerating! And *Good Morning* to you too!"

"My bad! I'm just saying. You know it bothers me when you don't answer my calls. And where you been all night?" Kesha's tone changed from concern to interrogation.

"I was in my bed, in my house, where I belong! Any more questions, Mrs. Officer?"

I rolled my neck and my eyes in unison, as though Kesha was standing in front of me. I didn't feel the need to explain why I was occupied last night. This morning is not the time to try my patience. Sometimes I swear this woman is in my life to make it more difficult.

Kesha continued speaking without taking a breath. She paused long enough to fire a few questions at me, and before I could respond, she answered for me. I often wondered if Kesha's motive for calling me was to hear herself speak. Eventually, I placed the phone on speaker mode as I organized my room and listened to Kesha's most recent drama. Once Kesha was out of breath and stopped drilling me, I knew she was tired of speaking.

"So, girl you down or what" Kesha said, more of a demand than a question.

"Kesha, what are you talking about?" I asked, sensing my aggravation reach its peak. Kesha had a bad habit of telling me instead of asking me. However, she has been my best friend since we were in grade school. How could I say no?

"Do you ever listen to me? I said me and Rob will be in Atlanta today. I will pick you up and we are going to the mall. Then you, me, Robert, and his friend will party tonight!" She was sure to speed up the ending of her sentence and place emphasis on every other word since she knew I would decline the offer.

"No, Kesha, I don't want to meet no more of Rob's friends, relatives, homeboys, or co-workers!" I sucked my teeth and sat down on the bed.

My last encounter with one of Roberts's friends was so disheartening, it forced me to break away from the dating scene. On that blind date, the dude had bad breath, yellow teeth, dirty shoes, dirt under his fingernails, and had the audacity to ask me to drive him home on our first date! I kindly got back in my car and pulled off; that was our first and last conversation. I truly want to meet someone, but I am far from desperate. I am content with being alone, most times silence is the norm, but never could equate to the feeling of loneliness. I try to give all men the benefit of the doubt, but a first impression is everything. If a man doesn't take pride in himself in the beginning, then I don't want any part of him in the end. Men are so comfortable nowadays with doing nothing, yet they expect everything in return.

"Hello? Are you there?" Kesha asked.

I zoned out and completely forgot to answer Kesha. I was busy thinking of different ways to decline her request. Kesha continued speaking.

"April, I promise you this guy is different. He is a homeowner, has a distinguished career, no kids, single, and no drama. He recently moved to Alabama. Please meet him?" Kesha whimpered, which aggravates the hell out of me when she begs.

"Okay, I will go out tonight. But, I promise you, Kesha, if this dude is a train wreck, you and Rob are going to regret you ever invited me out. And yes, I will go to the mall with you today but *you're* driving!"

"Yay! Trust me, girl, you won't regret it! And be ready at 3:00 p.m." Kesha got so excited that she dropped the phone, and hung up, without saying goodbye. Rude ass Kesha but I love her.

MR. UNKNOWN

"CURIOSITY CAN PEAK INTEREST OR CREATE DOUBTS."

I pinned my hair into a ponytail, squeezed into tight skinny jeans, and put on light make-up. I'm not in the mood to go shopping, and I don't plan on being out at the mall forever. My spaghetti strap, fitted shirt revealed just the right amount of skin. As I sat on the sofa, putting on my multi-colored pumps, my cell phone rang from inside of my bedroom. The noise my heels made on the hardwood floor, made me feel like an adult force of nature as I walked towards the bedroom. I had the usual gut feeling of who was calling, and to no surprise, Chris's number flashed across the screen. I held the phone in my hand, contemplating. Two thoughts crossed my mind: *answer or ignore the call*. I hate the fact that I make myself always so available to him. Before my fingers could swipe the green icon on the phone screen, the sound of the doorbell changed my decision. I hurriedly threw my cell phone in my purse, grabbed my keys, and walked towards the front door. *Saved by the bell* is all I could think to myself when I opened the front door. Kesha stood, impatiently tapping her foot, and playing with her fingernails.

"I thought I was going to have to grab my spare key with how long you were taking to answer the door!"

I laughed at Kesha while she was talking; she sure knows exactly how to start a good day.

"Girl, stop complaining before I turn around and walk back into my house and leave your miserable behind out here looking crazy. You better be glad I don't take you seriously sometimes." I walked past Kesha towards her car and didn't wait for her response. I figured one wasn't required right then, either way.

The ride to the mall was the usual; Kesha told me about how Robert continued pestering her regarding her delay to start a family.

"What is so wrong with your fiancé's request to start a family?" I stared at Kesha as she drove, hoping her facial expression would reflect her thoughts, but that didn't work.

"For one, I am not married to Robert, so at any given time, if he feels he can step out and leave me with a baby, then he can, and will. Secondly, I just think everything is right when you're married. Maybe I'm old school, but I just feel like marriage is more official." Kesha played with her sunglasses as she spoke.

"That's interesting, and I feel you, but please believe a ring won't keep your man faithful. A man will be faithful when he is ready to be faithful. Even with a ring, some men will get up and leave without thinking twice. Healthy relationships all surround effective communication, and learning about your spouse before you get married. Otherwise, you would invest time into a dead-end relationship." I said.

I often wondered why Kesha made a big deal about starting a family with Rob, whom she had dated for five years. Their relationship had withstood the test of time, endured infidelity, and other issues that would have ended most relationships. I honestly believe Kesha is afraid, but I thought it was best to save that conversation for another time.

The mall parking lot is jam-packed, and all Kesha continues to do is suck her teeth as she speeds up and down each aisle in the parking lot. Every area we drive past is either full, or the empty parking spot is too far of a walking distance from the mall entrance. I don't mind walking, but Kesha is not fond of working out or sweating. A few years ago, Kesha went on a strict diet and got her weight under control.

Kesha is shorter than me; she has a caramel complexion, her natural hair flows to the middle of her back, has thick firm thighs, and an apple bottom to match. To top everything off, Kesha is from the Virgin Islands. Most of the people I associate with are of Caribbean descent; it's not a preference, just always played out that way. We resemble sisters except for the height difference, and my smooth dark skin gives me a more exotic look.

After a few minutes of driving like a mad woman, with Kesha sucking her teeth while speaking her native language, we came to screeching halt. My neck whiplashed from the effect of Kesha stepping on the brakes so suddenly. I took my shades off and was just preparing to give Kesha the tongue-lashing of her life, when I heard a tap on the passenger side window. I looked up to see a man with bright yellow-teeth who couldn't have weighed more than one hundred pounds with a KINGS badge on his chest, staring at me. I grabbed onto my Beretta in my purse, prepared to pop fire in his ass. I don't give a damn who you are; I have an issue with strangers walking up on me, invading my personal space. The man noticed my seriousness, so he walked over to the driver's side door, flashing his butter smile at Kesha. Kesha put the car in park and fumbled through her purse, looking for something.

"Kesha, what are you doing?" I said.

"Meh can't tek de driving mess! And meh naah walk!" Kesha only speaks her native language when she's upset.

I just don't understand the need to rush. Kesha is not behaving as her normal self. It is weird to me, but nothing about Kesha is normal. The yellow-teeth man gently tapped on the driver's side window, waved, and smiled. For someone with such yellow teeth, he sure loved to show them. Kesha swung open her driver side door and almost knocked the skinny man down. Kesha handed the valet some money, took a ticket with a number on it from him, then looked at me and said, "Let's go." I shook my head, thinking to myself. *This girl done lost her mind! Valet parking at the mall? For real, though? I would never waste my money on valet parking at the mall unless it was something I could not avoid..*

All eyes were on us as we walked towards the mall entrance. My five-foot nine-inch frame, wearing four-inch pumps, combined with Kesha's hips and fluent accent, were bound to make heads turn and always brought attention.

"April, why are you walking so slow?" Kesha spoke with urgency.

Kesha is starting to get on my nerves. Between her road rage and this impatient attitude, I am tempted to snap. She noticed my look and sensed my patience was running thin.

"Okay, I'll stop with the attitude. In fact, I finally found the store I'm looking for." Kesha stopped in place like a blood hound.

I stopped next her and looked around, but didn't see any familiar stores that Kesha would normally shop in. Kesha walked towards the Athletic Footwear store. My shock was evident with my facial expression; *I could NEVER get Kesha to go into this type of store. Now I'm confused.* I stood at the entrance watching Kesha shop, it appeared she knew the exact type of sneaker she was looking for. That was my cue to shop for sneakers in the store. A woman like me can never have enough sneakers. I focused on my search for sneakers and hadn't noticed Kesha's prolonged absence. Kesha was in the Men's section, in deep conversation with someone. When she finally moved from blocking my view of the stranger, I almost dropped the sneaker I held in my hand. This man was handsome! He had to be nearly six feet three inches tall, nice, smooth dark complexion, shoulder-length locs, and the most alluring chestnut brown eyes. He caught me staring at him, so I quickly looked away.

Dammit I'm caught! But how does Kesha know this *man? I know he saw the diamond ring on her finger,* I thought to myself. I fondled a pair of shoelaces, hoping Kesha would finish up with her conversation soon, so we could leave. It is obvious they are familiar with each other, based on their body language. My thoughts were interrupted when Kesha walked over to me.

"Hey, you ready?" Kesha asked. She stared at me assuming I didn't see her conversing with the handsome man on the other side of the shoe store.

"Yeah, I'm ready, but I know you better answer my question. I didn't ask yet!" I said with my hands on my hips.

We laughed; I was ready to find out about this mystery man. My ringing cell phone interrupted my thoughts. I forgot I had my Bluetooth setting on automatic answer. I knew the familiar voice greeting me on the other end.

"Hi, Muma!" I loved talking to my mom when she didn't call me too much.

"Hey, my baby! Wha yuh ah do?" My mom lived in Jamaica and kept a heavy accent whenever she spoke.

"Meh ah watch Kesha spend all her money!" I looked over at Kesha and winked. Kesha heard me talking about her and slapped my arm while she snatched my phone. I disconnected the Bluetooth earpiece so she could speak to my mom on the cell phone.

"Hi, Mommy!" Kesha exclaimed.

I walked over to a pretzel stand, ordered my favorite cinnamon pretzel and a cup of water. Kesha and my mom were in deep conversation as my curiosity piqued about that man Kesha spoke to at the shoe store. For some odd reason, I could not get him off my mind. After Kesha and I walked the entire mall, a sense of satisfaction came over me, from having both our hands full of shopping bags. I was curious, but interested in the outcome of my date tonight. I had to admit, I was a little excited, but somewhat on edge because of my previous blind date experiences. This would be my final attempt to step out of the box to try the blind date thing again. The drive back home from the mall seemed way faster than the drive to the mall, probably because Kesha and I talked about the great sales we caught at the mall. The sun was setting when Kesha pulled into my driveway. I only had a few hours left before Kesha would be back to pick me up tonight. The cinnamon pretzel I ate at the mall earlier was a far memory, and my stomach rumbled for a more substantial meal. I fixed a nice chicken salad and drank a glass of sweet red wine to relax my nerves. I don't know where we are going tonight, but Kesha said to be prepared to eat and dance; which is all I needed to hear, since I love to do both. I had a few more sips of wine and got dressed for my special night. I hope I enjoy my date tonight.

TIME TO PARTY

"IF YOU DON'T TAKE A CHANCE ON YOURSELF...THEN WHO WILL?"

*T*he restaurant was beyond packed, with cars lined up in the parking lot and customers standing in line outside of the entrance. The smooth vibes of reggae music were heard from the entrance, and the spicy smell of jerk chicken caused my mouth water. There were many good-looking couples and singles waiting around to get a table inside the restaurant. I decided to wear my red bandage dress that pushed up my already perky breasts, and accentuated my shape. I wasn't fond of wearing this type of dress on a first date, but the number of stares I received from men and women alike proved me otherwise. I ran my hands down the sides of my hips to smooth the fabric out after sitting in the car.

"Girl, that dress is *bad*! He is going to love seeing you tonight," Kesha whispered in my ear. Kesha must have read my mind; we gave each other a high five. That spark of extra confidence was just what I needed to get through the night. I smiled at the thought of who *he* may be.

"Rob, table for four," the wavy-haired greeter yelled from the entrance. The greeter held the door open, looking around at the crowd waiting for us to come forward. *Wow, that was fast,* I thought. We only waited for ten minutes, while everyone else looked like they had been waiting for an hour.

Although Rob lives in Alabama, he has connections throughout Georgia so we rarely experienced long wait times at most restaurants. The restaurant is on the pier; our table was so close to the water that we could hear the water crashing along the side of the dam. I loved how the width of the table increased privacy on both sides. Although, Rob and Kesha sat directly across from me, I couldn't hear their conversation. The love between Rob and Kesha is evident, with how they treat each other, especially in public. I smiled as I watched them, with hopes of one day, sharing that same deep love for someone else, and it would be mutual.

Bob Marley's song, *Three Little Birds* played over the restaurant speakers. My body swayed to the music as I drank my piña colada. Bob Marley sang those words so well. I continued humming and singing along to the music. The warm night air caressed my skin. The cold piña colada kept my body at a perfect temperature as my mind relaxed to the sound of the reggae music. Either the drink was strong or I was in my zone, as I started to whine my hips in the booth, giving the soft cushion seat the ride of its life, until I felt someone tap my shoulder. I looked up and froze in surprise, as I stared into those same chestnut brown eyes I had seen earlier in the mall.

"Well, hello, beautiful. How are you doing? Is this seat taken?" He had the most welcoming smile; it pulled my body in but made me uncomfortable at the same time. His white teeth and manicured nails made it evident that he took pride in the way he looked. I took a quick glance at his slacks, which were creased, and his loafers were clean as well. I love a confident, kempt man. He passed the hygiene test, so I scooted over and made room for him to sit next to me. He looked over at me after he was seated.

"Thank you, beautiful. I would love to continue to call you by that name because it suits you well. But I would rather ask you for your name before I choose names for you. My name is Ahmad, and yours?"

Ahmad held his hand out for me to shake. I can't believe this man is bold enough to sit next to me in front of my friends, then talk to me and ask questions. It appears he had been invited here. He held his hand out, awaiting my shake of approval. I contemplated his true intentions. *I hope this man is not a stalker.* Rob and Kesha noticed my not-so- friendly attitude and their voices intercepted the awkwardness between Ahmad and I, which almost bubbled over.

"What's good, Maad?" they said in unison.

"Nothing much. I missed y 'all, and the ride here was nothing nice. I forgot how crazy traffic is in Atlanta, but it was all worth it." Ahmad looked at me, winked, and got up and hugged Kesha and Rob. By now, I was extremely confused and hoped my drink would clear my mind. I took another sip of my drink which was two sips away from being finished.

"Okay, so let me get this straight. You all know one another?" I raised my eyebrows, while looking back and forth between the three of them.

"Yes, April. Remember the date I was telling you about? Well, this is Ahmad, Rob's best friend. You have never met or heard about him because he was always traveling and playing football.

Ahmad lives in Alabama now, and I'm sure he can explain the rest of his life story on y 'all time not mine," Kesha said.

I finished my drink and gave Kesha the evil eye. I was not happy. Kesha not only set this blind date up so awkwardly, but had also kept this fine man a secret from me this long. Rob and Ahmad engaged in conversation as I listened to Kesha explain herself yet again.

"Girl, he is fioonne. I am so nervous, but I am not stupid or desperate. Just because he is Rob's best friend doesn't mean he is the man for me." I couldn't finish my sentence before Kesha interrupted me.

"April, stop acting like you're in a relationship or something. You're always holding back, and I don't know what for? Maad is a gentleman; just give him a chance. Stop closing doors that are trying to open, and stop leaving doors open that need to remain closed." Kesha looked at me with pleading eyes, and from across the table, placed her hand on top of mine.

Kesha is familiar with my past experiences, but I wasn't sure if she would understand my present situation. I also wasn't ready to reveal it to her yet. I felt the need to hold back because I was waiting…waiting for what? I don't know. So how could she understand why I felt so nervous? The guys stopped talking, and both looked our way, waiting for us to tell them the next move. Kesha gave me a wink, kissed Rob, and then they excused themselves from our table and walked towards the end of the pier. I ordered a second drink and Ahmad ordered a rum and coke with a basket of several types of fried seafood appetizers. The awkward silence was driving me crazy; I thought about my impolite first impression, and I knew I needed to do something to change it, fast.

"So, Ms. Beautiful, I still did not receive your name. Or can I continue to call you beautiful?" Ahmad was determined, and I was attracted to his confidence. I tried not to blush but I couldn't help it.

"My name is April. It is very nice to meet you, Ahmad. I apologize for my silence earlier; I'm just not used to blind dates," I said.

I wanted to tell him my reasoning behind my thoughts, but I froze because his sexy-ass eyes had me in a trance. There is a special connection there that I can't explain at the moment.

"It's cool, April. I'm not either, and to be honest, I was very nervous about this date, and even more nervous after I met you. This is my first blind date. Not really blind because I saw you at the mall earlier." He winked and smiled at me.

Now, everything became clearer to me. Kesha rushed to the mall so Ahmad and I could see each other before we met, without knowing who we both were. She knew we would be attracted to each other, but she wanted to see for herself. *My sneaky friend is something else.* The food arrived, and our conversation flowed. There were no silent or awkward moments. I learned Ahmad had a few serious relationships in the past, but they all never worked out. The issues ranged from trust, distance, and communication, to respect. He was engaged to the last woman he had dated, who ultimately broke his heart. I know there are always three sides to every story, but the way his last relationship played out would have broken anyone's heart. He changed his entire lifestyle to suit his ex-fiancée but later found out the feelings weren't mutual. She chose her family over him because her parents did not feel Ahmad was a good enough provider for their daughter. I could tell it hurt Ahmad deeply just from the way he explained his past relationship. She did not want him when he wasn't famous or didn't have much money. I felt bad for the hurt he experienced but was glad he had the courage to move forward.

I firmly believe if someone cannot be with you while you're down, then you don't need them around when you move up. He explained to me how important it is for mutual respect between a woman and man. Ahmad believed in treating his lady like a Queen and allowing her to be the woman in the relationship, not the man. I loved his thought process and enjoyed listening to him speak. I had never met a man who voluntarily revealed personal information, and I didn't have to ask. It appeared we were on the same page with every subject.

He paused momentarily and asked me about my past, and what I was looking for in a man or relationship. I kept my answers short and sweet. Although I was comfortable with him, I wasn't ready to reveal everything on our first date.

We continued to eat and drink throughout the night until the restaurant turned into a dance club. The restaurant opened a dance floor area in front of a stage. A live band came out, and the performance was amazing. The atmosphere was relaxing and the energy from the crowd boiled over onto the dance floor. The band played all the hottest reggae and dancehall songs. I almost felt like I was at a live concert. Ahmad noticed me swaying my body to the beat in my seat, moving like a seat dancer.

"I see you are enjoying yourself in that seat, huh. You scared to get on the dance floor?" Ahmad smiled.

"I actually am, but..." I hesitated.

"But, you want to dance. I had to finish that sentence for you. You are looking way too beautiful tonight and I must show you off. Would you like to dance with me?" Ahmad said.

"Of course!" I placed my hand in his as he led me to the dance floor.

Everyone stared at us as we swayed to the beat on the dance floor. I guess between our heights and our outfits, we probably would have won the best couple award if they had one. This was the first man who could hold my entire body in his arms. I felt safe and secure. I grinded my hips into his groin and felt his hands rest on my thighs. I was enjoying myself and didn't care who was watching. The band performed, *No Ordinary Love* by Alaine. It was as though the DJ read my mind as I danced to the first verse of the song. Everything felt so perfect and normal, all on the first date. Ahmad turned me around and ran the back of his hand gently along the side of my face. Our eyes locked, and it was as though he saw right through me. His eyes told me I could trust him and I should trust him, but I needed confirmation from my heart. While he cuddled my face in his large hands, he leaned in and passionately kissed me. His tongue traveled the inside of my mouth, and I imagined how it would feel between my legs. Caught up in the vibe, I didn't care that we were in the middle of the dance floor or that I hadn't seen Kesha and Rob since they left us at the table. What mattered to me in that moment was my future with Ahmad. After our first kiss, the music sped up and women started to Dutty Whine in the middle of the dance floor. As I leaned my back against his chest, Ahmad held onto my hips and rested his head on my shoulder, watching the women dance like they were in a competition.

"April, it's getting late and I don't want to keep you out all night. Are you ready to go?" Ahmad didn't have to yell over the music; my ears are already in tune with his voice.

"Yes, I am ready but where are Kesha and Rob?" A few hours had passed since they left the table and I didn't receive any call or text from Kesha. Ahmad noticed the concerned expression on my face.

"Rob texted me earlier and told me that he wanted us to enjoy our night and him and Kesha headed back to their hotel."

I was surprised. The least Kesha could have done was call or text me. *Yeah, leave it to Kesha to keep up with surprises*, I thought.

"Okay, that's fine. Well, I am getting a little drowsy, so we can leave if you are ready to go." Ahmad nodded and grabbed my hand as I followed him through the crowd of people on the dance floor.

We walked towards the entrance of the restaurant. Ahmad handed the valet a ticket, and one of the workers spoke over the radio. Within a few minutes, Ahmad's car pulled up to the entrance. We walked up to the black Mercedes Benz G550; he opened the passenger side door and held my hand as I sat down. The cushioned seats and crème leather interior welcomed my body. I felt every ache and pain from moving my body on the dance floor; it had been a work-out.

I looked around the interior of the car while I watched Ahmad walk to the driver's side. Not only could this man dress, but he also took care of everything he had, which revealed to me he didn't take anything for granted. A humble man is always a good man. I looked at Ahmad but wasn't sure if I felt comfortable enough for him to take me home. I wasn't fond of strangers knowing where I live, especially on the first date. However, Ahmad basically was family, so I tried not to worry too much. On the drive to my house, I was so deep in thought; I didn't notice the smile on my face.

"Well, someone looks very happy. I hope I played a role in that matter." Ahmad rubbed my hand and smiled.

I felt like I could get used to this type of treatment and the bliss that came along with being in a happy, committed relationship. When we pulled up to my house, I noticed the expression on his face. Most people are surprised when they see my house because it is very spacious for one person. My four-bedroom, five-bathroom home, with a two-car garage and one-acre lot is my place of peace.

From everything I've been through in my life, I deserved the best. I haven't had the worst life, but I earned everything I have. I also appreciate what I receive. I truly believe if I take care of the little that I have, my blessings will increase. All my life I felt the need to save my money so I could take care of myself, or others if needed. The least I could do is have a peaceful spot where I could rest my mind, body, and spirit.

Ahmad pulled his car into the driveway, parked, and walked outside to open the passenger side door. I placed my hands in his as he helped me out of his car. My feet burned from dancing in heels all night, but the pain was worth it. We walked to my front door in silence. I didn't want the night to end, but for some odd reason, I knew this was just the beginning.

"I had a great night, April, but this is only the beginning," Ahmad said with confidence.

"Is that so? What makes you so sure this won't be the last?" I tilted my head to the side and placed my hand on my hip.

"A man knows when he has found a treasure, and you're definitely my diamond. In time, we will both see, only if you allow me to."

Ahmad lifted my hand to his face and kissed the palm of my hand. My heart melted, but I couldn't show that to him, not on the first date. I didn't know what to say, or if his comments even required a response. Ahmad leaned in for a hug and a good night kiss. The pleasant aroma of his cologne and the firmness of his touch tempted me. I didn't want to let him go.

"Goodnight, beautiful. I will call you tomorrow," Ahmad said.

"Okay, love. I had a wonderful time with you tonight. Drive safe."

We kissed before I turned away to walk into my house. I felt his gaze burn into my back as I made an extra effort to swish my hips. To say my night was great is an understatement.

AHMAD

Beauty Is Her Name, by Dru Hill is the only song that comes to mind since the day April came into my life. When Rob called a few months ago and told me Kesha had a best friend who was single, I didn't think anything of it. I questioned why Kesha hadn't told me herself. I assumed it was because I was always traveling. Before I was drafted into the NFL and relocated to Philadelphia, I dated Nadine, whom I thought was the woman of my dreams. I knew I wanted to spend the rest of my life with her. We were engaged, but we weren't living together. I did everything right by her, but the day she broke off the engagement is when I realized the love she had for me was a lie. Her parents didn't feel I had the financial stability they desired for their daughter, so Nadine broke off the engagement and wished me well. What hurt me the most was I loved her for who she was, not for what she could offer me. I had changed everything about myself to suit her needs.

As a man, being a provider is something I take pride in. It took me a while to get over her. The pain I felt only motivated me to push harder physically, mentally, financially, and emotionally. Nadine continued to try to remain in my life as a friend, especially when she saw how much I progressed financially and physically, but I no longer felt her love was genuine. Although I have ignored Nadine attempts to contact me. Nadine still calls me and sends holiday cards and letters through the mail to my mother, but none of her efforts fazes me. I just don't want anything to do with her anymore. The end of that relationship was a big blow to my heart, but I used that time to relocate and reevaluate myself. I will never compromise my integrity for anyone ever again; if a woman cannot love me for who I am or what I have to offer as a man, then she can keep it moving. That is my mentality.

A few months ago, I notified Rob about my NFL contract termination and my injury settlement agreement. I completed physical rehabilitation and planned my move back to my hometown Birmingham, Alabama. Rob lives in Tuscaloosa, not too far from Birmingham. Rob was ecstatic about the news of my relocation. He is like a brother to me; we've been there for each other through everything since we were kids. While I drove from Philadelphia to Alabama, Rob called me and asked that I meet Kesha at the Athletic Footwear store inside of the Lennox Mall in Atlanta, Georgia, since he and Kesha were visiting there. I had a few weeks to spare before my business in Birmingham was up and running, so it would only make sense for me to enjoy myself. I thought it was funny how Rob always mentioned how Kesha loved surprising others, so I was game to see what she had up her sleeve this time.

During much of my drive to Atlanta, I listened to a few excerpts I downloaded to my media player of Dr. Umar Johnson. He spoke about the importance of family bonds within the black community. While others may find it boring, listening to a motivational speaker during a road trip, I find it quite interesting and educational. There is a major breakdown of unity within the black community segregating the love to be shared among one another. The African-American man is not aware of his role in society, and, therefore, is led astray, due to the lack of guidance and support within his community. I am determined to be a strong representation of what the African-American man can do within the community, while I hope to inspire young brotha's to achieve those dreams as well.

As I turned into the Lennox Mall parking lot, it was difficult to find a parking spot; cars were everywhere, just no place to park. After circling the parking lot for a few minutes, I finally noticed a minivan pull out of a parking spot in front of me. The female driver turned wildly, as she yelled at a group of rambunctious kids in her backseat to sit down and watch for other cars as she backed out of her parking spot. One of the unruly kids in the passenger seat, who couldn't be any older than ten years old, flicked a bird at me, while the other child in the back seat smeared her face against the window and stuck her finger in her nose. I shook my head as I pulled into the parking spot, thinking about the scene I had just witnessed with the kids in the minivan. It consistently disappoints me when I come across parents who are unwilling to discipline their kids, especially when those children represent our future generation. The parking spot wasn't far from the mall entrance. When I walked into the mall, I noticed the Athletic Footwear store sign advertising a sneaker sale. I exhaled at the thought of how busy the store was, and I hadn't planned on spending money unnecessarily. I don't understand why Kesha chose this store out of all the stores in the mall to meet up. I walked in and looked at a few sneakers, and then I felt a tap on my shoulder, forcing me to turn around.

"So, I see you found something you like?" I recognized the voice.

"Hey, Keesh! What's up?" We hugged. Although I considered Kesha as Rob's wife, she is more of a little sister to me and I felt an obligation to protect her as such.

"Nothing much, just wanted to get out the house and check the mall out for a few. How was your drive?" Kesha asked.

"My drive wasn't bad at all. I didn't run into much traffic until I got to Atlanta. Enough about me, though. What's the real reason behind this invitation?" I asked.

"Well, if you must know, Robert and I are going out tonight and we would like for you to join us. I have a blind date set up for you." Kesha had a big Kool-Aid smile on her face.

"I don't know about the blind date thing, Kesha. It's been a while since I've been on a date, let alone a blind date."

"Come on, Ahmad, please consider it. I promise you won't regret it. Just try, and if you don't like your date you won't have to worry about me asking you to do this ever again." Kesha put her hands behind her back, looking up at me like an innocent little girl, knowing she is the total opposite of innocent.

"All right, I will be there tonight. I need to get out anyway."

I noticed Kesha looking over at a woman on the opposite side of the store. When the woman turned and looked our way, I froze. She was breathtaking. There was a natural aura surrounding her body, drawing me into her deep brown eyes. Women who embrace their natural beauty, without wearing pounds of make-up, are the women I find most attractive. Kesha caught me staring at the woman across the store and smiled. As soon as the woman and I locked eyes, she turned around, possibly shy or embarrassed. I was confused as to why she looked away so suddenly.

"Ahmad, Ahmad, are you there? Why do you have that confused look on your face?" Kesha asked. Kesha looked up at me, waving her hand as I was in a daze.

"Yes, do you know that woman?" I asked Kesha.

I was now very curious and continued staring at the other woman's direction although she didn't look my way anymore.

"I sure do, but anyway, I have to go. Glad that you came here. Enjoy shopping, and we will catch you later!" Kesha winked and smiled.

She walked to the other side of the store, quickly grabbed the unknown woman by the arm, and then they both walked out of the store. When I saw April again later that night at the restaurant, I was surprisingly overjoyed that I was given the opportunity to see the woman I connected with earlier today. My night with April was amazing; there was something inside of April drawing me closer to her. I wanted to learn more about her, but it appears she was holding back. Whenever children or family was mentioned, her face brightened and turned cold in the same moment. April had a delicate heart that I could tell she kept protected. I am determined to learn about her present and future, especially her past that she won't seem to reveal.

APRIL

Six Months Later…

Over these past few months, Ahmad and I have been rocking hard. I opened up to Ahmad and revealed just about everything to him, and I didn't regret doing it at all. Every other weekend we'd travel to spend time with each other; I was either in Alabama or him in Georgia. Most of the time I'd visit him, since my job was more flexible. As a financial advisor, I set my work schedule; a great benefit of being a business owner. Many of my clients were athletes and business owners so I didn't have a typical 9:00 a.m. – 5:00 p.m. work schedule. When I was away, my secretary made sure everything ran smoothly, as though I were there. A few months ago, Ahmad and I agreed to be exclusive. I was vulnerable around Ahmad, and the feeling made me nervous at times, but I was ready to move forward and let go of my past. Not only did I love him, but every day I fell deeper in love with him. It was difficult for me to reveal my greatest secret. In due time, I knew that I needed to acknowledge the truth, and so would he. I was caught up in my thoughts and I didn't hear my office desk phone ringing. I grabbed it in time.

"April speaking, how can I help you?"

The voice on the other end created knots in my stomach that caused my heart to flutter.

"Hey, April! I know you've been doing your thing and what not, but I wanted you to know that I miss you and think about you all the time."

Although I hate to admit it, hearing Chris's voice on the phone brought back good memories. I hadn't spoken to Chris in months, forcing myself to move on. During our last conversation, I broke down and revealed to Chris that I had met someone and I wanted to see where it went. I didn't want to cloud my mind or heart with an unavailable man. I knew Chris cared for me, and was hurt by that statement, but I couldn't deal with his situation much longer. He had no choice but to allow me to do me. At the end of the day, my happiness is what matters to me the most.

I hesitated to speak, fearing I'd say the wrong thing.

"I am doing well, Chris, just trying to finish up this report for Jonathan," I said.

Jonathan is my most demanding and lucrative client; he also referred many of my clients. Basically, if Jonathan asked me for something at the last minute, it would get done, even it meant I had to work longer than normal hours.

"Well, I know that will keep you busy, but not all night. It's Friday! Let's shoot pool tonight, or we can catch a movie and have drinks if you want. I miss you, April, even as a friend," Chris said.

I sensed the sincerity in Chris's voice, and I missed him too. I wanted to fight the urge to see him, but in the end, Chris was a good friend to me and was there for me through the worst. The thought of us hanging out shouldn't be a problem.

"Sure, Chris we can hang out. You can pick me up around 9:00 p.m." I exhaled and tried to sound aggravated, even though I was far from both.

"Great! I knew I would be driving your lazy butt around anyway," Chris joked. Anyone who understood me, knows that I don't like driving locally but I would not hesitate to drive long distances or take road trips.

"All right, well, I will see you later." My excitement was hidden in my voice.

"Cool. See you soon, A," Chris said.

Chris always called me by my nickname. I sensed Chris's excitement, though I couldn't see his face. I am constantly amazed at how well we understand each other. I pulled open my desk drawer and felt around for the tiny, velvet- textured box. I fondled the cute, black ribbon bow tied on top of the little box. I opened the box and glared at the two-carat princess cut diamond ring glistening from the reflection of the office lights. Staring at the ring brought back memories of the past.

...Two Years Ago...

I continued my daily routine, work, gym, then home. I enjoyed working out, it was a true stress reliever, but lately I had grown tired of working out alone. Each gym visit, I entered the gym as though I had tunnel vision, and my focus was getting in and getting out, but this day was different. As I walked through the gym doors, the smell of sweat mixed with chlorine attached to my nostrils. The scent reminded me of an indoor pool.

There was always the short, stocky gym trainer who greeted everyone at the door. His arms looked like he struggled to get them into his shirt, and his veins were the size of shoelaces; he resembled a character out of a Marvel comic book. I smiled and walked past the mini Hulk, making my way upstairs to the cardio room. My headphones were in my ears, blasting the hottest pop and rap music to get me hyped for my workout. I pressed the plus and minus signs on the machine to adjust the incline and difficulty levels while my legs moved faster on the elliptical machine.

Someone got on the machine next to me, and everything in my body cringed. My greatest pet peeve at the gym is when there are plenty of empty machines but someone chooses to get on the machine next to me. I glanced over and could tell it was a man, but I didn't bother to look any further or make it obvious that I was staring. After a few minutes, the sweat poured down my face, neck, and back. Once the initial shock of not properly warming up went away, my muscles relaxed and my breathing was more controlled.

I imagined running on a track, the sun beating down on my skin. The shiny reflection of the salt, sweat, and the sun bouncing off my skin gave it a smooth sensual look. I enjoyed reflecting on my younger days when I competed in track and field. Those thoughts motivated me during my gym workouts. I moved my legs faster on the elliptical until my time was up on the machine. My stopwatch on my wrist went off, signaling my cue to move to the next portion of my work-out on the weight machine. After my workout, I was drenched in sweat. I walked into the sauna to relax my muscles. The only person in the sauna was an older woman, butt-naked with saggy breasts and wrinkly skin, sitting with her legs open for everyone to see. Unfortunately, I was the only one in the sauna with this woman.

Although, I sat facing the opposite direction, the thought of what I had seen haunted my mind like a nightmare. Why was this woman sitting in the sauna in her birthday suit for everyone to see? And why did she have her legs open? The thoughts grossed me out; all that madness was my sign that it was time for me to leave the gym. The craziest part of that random situation was that the woman had smiled at me when I walked towards the door to get out of the sauna. All I could do was shake my head in disgust when I walked out of the sauna. After I left the gym, I went next door to the smoothie shop and sat near the window, drinking my smoothie; blueberry, apple, strawberry, banana, and spinach mix is my favorite. I sat staring out the window as everyone walked to and from their cars in the parking lot. Sometimes I enjoy wondering what other people are thinking or where they were going. The cold and tasty smoothie gave me the right amount of energy my body needed after a hard workout. My thoughts were quickly interrupted.

"Excuse me, is that seat vacant?"

I looked up at this tall, dark-skinned, bald, handsome man with brown almond colored eyes and the most beautiful smile. When he turned to the side, I saw dimples that gave him an innocent look; even *I* knew that looks can be deceiving.

"Yes, it is. You can sit there if you'd like," I said.

I was sitting alone so I didn't mind the company. I looked out the window while he took the seat across from me.

"I appreciate it. By the way, my name is Chris, and yours?" He held out his hand across from the table.

"No problem, it's not like I own this place. My name is April. Nice to meet you, Chris." My hand connected with his, as we laughed in unison.

"If you don't mind me asking, why do you stare out the

window? All I see is a bunch of people in the hot sun, walking back and forth in a busy parking lot full of cars," Chris said.

"Well, when I look out the window, I am looking for the smaller details that many people do not notice. Do you see that bird on the top of the light post in the parking lot looking down for prey? How about that woman holding her child's hand as they cross the street? Do you see the couple over there kissing, leaning against the car?" As I spoke, I pointed to each location in the parking lot.

"Oh, wow, I didn't even notice any of that. That's actually interesting to me that you notice all those details." Chris stared out of the window with me, as he looked for specific details.

"Yeah, well, it all goes back to my philosophy that there is always a bigger picture to everything. I'm glad I could enlighten you, though." I smiled and winked at Chris as I drank my smoothie.

"That you did! Speaking of details, I see you work out at the gym religiously. I noticed you a while ago, but each time I tried to catch you to speak, you were gone. It was as though when you entered the gym, you were on a mission and no one could stop you!" We chuckled.

"I recently noticed that about myself, so I tried to change it up today and be a little more observant … until I had an unpleasant experience in the sauna…" My eyes widened as I continued to speak. "So, I had a great workout and walked into the sauna to relax, but why was my first view an older naked woman with her legs spread open staring into space as if she was in a room alone?" I shook my head in disgust at the thought of it all.

Chris laughed uncontrollably as I described my experience.

"That is too funny! But I see it often in the men's locker room. Some of these older guys have no shame and let it all hang out.

They don't care who is around, so I feel your pain, April. I wish I could cover my eyes when I walk in the locker room sometimes, but then I would probably bump into everything, and the last thing I want to bump into with my eyes closed is another naked man." Chris smiled.

We talked for hours, the conversation flowed naturally. This was our first outing of many. For the next few months, I rarely worked out alone at the gym. Chris and I went from workout partners to close friends. At the time that I met Chris, I was in a rocky relationship with Ricky. Eventually I knew our relationship would end. When I met Ricky, he pulled out all the tricks he could to impress me. He showed me that he loved me until he finally had me. Once I took the bait, everything else slowly went out the window, especially after I found out that I was pregnant. After the initial shock, everything in my life moved in slow motion. I no longer wanted to be with Ricky, but he continuously declared his love for me and his desire for us to work it out as a family. *The typical things men say to get women back.*

Ricky never seemed to get it right, and I grew tired of hearing the same story about supposedly old girlfriends popping up in his current life. The old girlfriends were either fuck friends or hoes or everything under the sun, but what I saw proved me otherwise. Sex buddies, or whatever they're called nowadays, should not know your family nor share any emotional ties. Obviously, Ricky had different definitions, which I chose not to put up with. I also believed that if a man can't be faithful, then at least he should give the woman the courtesy of deciding if she wants to be with him or not. That's the problem nowadays; men don't know how to keep their side chicks in place. Back in the day, the side chick knew her role and played it well, while the man treated his lady with respect. Today, the side chicks don't know their role, disrespecting the man and his lady, making private pictures public, and doing everything else whores usually do. Sad state of mind that these young girls think is normal, and it's even worse when the man allows it.

As time went on and my belly grew bigger, Ricky's words were so far from the truth that I believed I was living a lie. Between the stress of my relationship, my pregnancy, my career, and everything else, many times I found myself lonely and exhausted.

While I contemplated my relationship with Ricky, Chris remained by my side every step of the way. Chris worked out with me at the gym while I was pregnant, even though I knew it hindered his usual routine. He never showed me that it inconvenienced him. Not only was this my first pregnancy, but I didn't live near my family and was a good distance away from my close friends. He was there when I was four weeks pregnant and considering an abortion, up until I decided to woman up and take care of my own. I contacted several abortion clinics and compared different prices to abort a baby, but I couldn't gain the courage to go through with it. I promised myself that if I could lie down and not use protection then I needed to be prepared to handle what occurred afterwards. The thought of ending the life growing inside of me sent an ocean of tears my way.

I wasn't sure that I could carry a pregnancy, due to my medical issues, and after I conceived, I knew it was a blessing from God, so why would I want to destroy it? The embarrassment, combined with the prospective career opportunities I would have to postpone because of my pregnancy, flooded my thoughts. Just because I had those opportunities didn't mean I would succeed; there is no guarantee for what could be when it has not happened yet. I couldn't abort my unborn child for a job or a man. It was time for me to think about someone else other than myself.

I made up my mind, and was ready to start this journey alone. I couldn't continue stressing over Ricky and trying to raise a man who acted like a boy. The stress was draining me physically and emotionally until I decided to let it go and move forward with my life. I eventually broke up with Ricky while I was pregnant, and focused on my future and the future of my unborn child. At twelve weeks pregnant, Ricky never made it to even one doctor's appointment. One characteristic about me is my resiliency. I am always prepared for everything, and the prospect of being a single mother was no different. I created a savings account for my baby and moved forward with living my life without my child's father around.

As time progressed, so did my excitement with giving birth. Chris saw my pain and was there with me through the tears, and as much as I wanted Chris to beat the breaks off Ricky, I had to restrain Chris from doing so. Chris told me he started looking at baby clothes and was waiting to know the sex before he went shopping. I looked at Chris as a friend, but sometimes I wished it was Chris's baby I was carrying and not Ricky's. I knew I was having a boy, and didn't need an ultrasound to confirm my feeling. I was not hoping for a boy or girl but it was like my spirit was telling me I have a baby boy growing inside of me.

I was raised in a spiritual family, and my family would call and pray with me often over the phone. Each prayer gave me strength, especially when I was told that this baby would be my blessing. The first time I saw this new life growing inside of me was at fourteen weeks. The doctor took an ultrasound picture for me to keep of the baby. I could clearly see every image of my baby through the ultrasound. The doctor was amazed at how well-developed my son appeared. Every night I would rub my belly while I sang and spoke to my son; those were the only times I felt at peace. The first time I felt him move was at fifteen weeks, and it was a truly amazing feeling. I knew he was going to be a big healthy baby. That is exactly what the doctors said, and based on the ultrasound, that is what I believed.

Although I hadn't given birth yet, I already loved my son and made sure he felt it and knew it. Everything was running smoothly with my pregnancy, and I slowly got back in motion after the break-up. I had my normal routine checkup at seventeen weeks.

During each appointment, the protocol is to do an ultrasound to check on the baby. So, as the doctor pulled out the machine, I lay on my back and flinched as she rubbed the cold jelly along the bottom of my stomach. The ultrasound handle had a ball on the end that rolled along the skin and captured video clips of the baby through ultrasound waves. The doctor rolled the handle around for what seem like forever. After a few minutes, an alarmed expression came to her face. She asked me to lie on my side, being that babies were stubborn sometimes and didn't want to move, and she rolled the handle around my belly again. I didn't understand what she was looking for or why she looked concerned.

"I'm looking for a heartbeat, ma'am. Have you experienced any recent trauma?" the doctor asked with a curious expression. By this time, my heart was beating extremely fast and I knew something was not right.

"No trauma at all. As a matter of fact, everything has been normal for the past few days. Is something wrong?" I asked. My palms were sweaty and I felt extremely nervous. The doctor's eyes saddened.

"Ma'am, I'm sorry..."

"What do you mean *you're* sorry? I don't understand?" I tried to control the pitch of my voice. These hormones were outrageous sometimes. Her sadness made me sit up, and I didn't care that my pants were still unbuckled and my belly was showing. I needed to know what she was talking about.

"Ma'am, I'm sorry for your loss. Your baby's heart is no longer beating, and if you had not come in today, your body would have eventually aborted the baby at any moment, which could have been dangerous and a horrific experience for you. Since you didn't have any signs of trauma, I cannot calculate how long ago the fetus passed away, so I need to admit you into the hospital as soon as possible, and we must induce your labor so you can deliver. I know this is a lot for you to handle right now, but you can go home and pack your things and call us when you're ready to be admitted tonight. We will have a room prepared for you and available for your loved ones. I can send a counselor in right now if you'd like me to or give you a moment alone..." Her voice trailed off.

She couldn't fully finish her statement before I released a loud wail. The shock, the hurt, and the pain hit me at once. The doctor rubbed my shoulder as I cried for what felt like an eternity. I allowed the doctor to excuse herself until I gathered what emotions were left of me at the time. With cloudy red eyes as puffy as a blowfish, I drove home, sat on the couch for the next hour, and stared at the wall in silence.

The beating of my heart and my thoughts were all I could hear. Listening to my heart beat brought tears to my eyes, knowing that my unborn son was dead inside of me. I sent a few text messages to my family members and close friends, notifying them of my situation, and avoided their phone calls afterwards. I didn't want to talk to anyone, not even God. I called Ricky and let him know what was going on. I could hear the sadness in his voice, but I could care less at that moment, considering he didn't do much to help me during my pregnancy. A few hours later, Kesha picked me up and brought me to the hospital. I made sure Kesha and Ricky didn't arrive at the same time because they never got along, and Kesha was at her breaking point with him. So was I, but the hospital wasn't the time or the place for the drama. I removed my sweatpants and T-shirt and put on the paper-thin hospital gown before I sat on the hospital bed. Kesha kept me company at the hospital for a few hours, then she left, since Ricky was on his way. After Ricky arrived, an older nurse walked into the room and explained the different medications that she would be administering to me. She told me she would insert a pill inside of my vagina that would force my cervix to dilate and I would experience cramping from the sensation of my body being forced into premature labor. I declined the epidural and was in labor for the next eight hours.

Over the next eight hours, I prayed for some sort of miracle to happen and that God would allow me to deliver a healthy baby boy, crying out with life and waiting on his mother's love. Perhaps my son's heart would beat, and everything would return to normal; maybe the doctors were making a mistake. Unfortunately, when the doctors took a third ultrasound picture the moment before they administered the pill to me, I knew I was living in denial. My son was not moving, and there was no heartbeat. The nurse apologized once again before she administered the vaginal pill, and life, as I knew it, was over for me.

At 8:38 a.m. the next morning, after I grunted, screamed, and pushed the lifeless body outside of me, I delivered my first and only baby boy. The first words I heard from the midwife was, "It's a boy!" Those words were far from joyous in my mind. I couldn't control the tears or the fact that the nurse was digging her hands inside of my vagina after she handed me my baby boy, wrapped in a blanket. After more labs were drawn from me and my son, I spent the next ten hours in the hospital, holding him and counting all ten of his fingers and toes. Ricky was there with me while I delivered, and he held my hand and cried during the entire process. I never understood why he was crying, but I knew that moment marked the end for us. I loved Ricky, but he wasn't ready to love me the way I needed to be loved. We named our son after his father; his nickname was RJ. After RJ's death certificate was signed, we were given a memorial box full of RJ's blankets, hat, and socks.

I spent half of the day in the hospital holding my son, then I knew it was time for me to let him go. I kissed his face and chest, looked at him one last time, and then handed RJ over to the nurse, who stood with tears in her eyes. The most challenging times for me were the days that followed. I couldn't eat, I didn't sleep, and my breasts lactated with no baby around. For the next few days, I used a napkin on the inside of my bra until my breasts stopped lactating. My body was sore, my mind tired, and I was alone. Ricky completely disappeared, and I was at the lowest point of my life. I thought the worst was over until a week later, I felt extremely sick and my body was weaker than normal. I was admitted into the emergency room, and found out that one of the nurses who had assisted with the delivery of my son did not do a suitable job of ensuring the entire placenta was intact, post-delivery. In turn, I suffered a deadly infection that required surgery. During my post-surgery recovery, Kesha, a few of my co-workers, and Chris visited me. I lay in the hospital bed, depressed once again, with different questions going through my mind.

Why did God make me the laughing stock? I always did everything right in my life, even if I had to suffer, but why was I always tortured? Does it matter to be honest and caring anymore? Why do I have to be strong for everyone else and myself?

～

*N*ow, sitting in my office, I had not realized that I was crying until the tears fell on the little box that I held in my hand. After I went through that traumatic experience in my life, Chris bought me this two-carat princess cut diamond ring and promised he would always be there for me and would remain open and honest with me. I have never met a man who showed such genuine love to me and didn't ask for anything in return. Not only did Chris earn my respect, but he also earned my love, that I'd hidden away for so long. The tears blurred my vision, almost causing the ring box to slip from my tight grasp. I pulled a handkerchief from the desk drawer to pat my eyes and face. It was not a clever idea to mess up my make-up while I was at work. *Never let 'em see you sweat,* I thought to myself. I closed the ring box and placed it inside the drawer before I left my office.

CHRIS

I was going through withdrawal, I hadn't seen April in six months. I not only missed April as my lover, but also as my friend. I thought about our last conversation where she referred to me as an unavailable man. Those words stung like boiling water. I don't know what hurt the most—the truth of those words or the fact that it came out of her mouth. I knew exactly why she felt the way the way she did, and I knew it would only be a matter of time before that day would come. After we ended our phone conversation, I gazed at April's contact picture in my phone and reflected back years ago when I finally revealed the truth.

A pril and I were steady friends for almost a year, and everything was going great. I never believed that a man could have a platonic relationship with a woman until I met April.

Being with April felt easy, and nothing was forced; our conversation was always entertaining, and I enjoyed spending time with her even if we sat around in silence. April's presence alone kept me at peace. I was always there for April, and she knew how important she was to me. I loved this woman, and she made it easy to do so. As our friendship grew stronger, so did our attraction to each other. There were awkward moments where I'd fall asleep at her house and wake up with a hard-on or she would forget I was there and walk out of her bathroom naked, and run back into her bathroom from embarrassment. There were also other moments where we would hold hands longer than normal or stare at each other longer than normal. The attraction was real and undeniable. At that time, I wasn't sure if taking our friendship to the next level was the right decision. Sometimes I would stare at her as she slept on my chest; she would look so peaceful, my little angel.

It was a rainy day, so I invited April to my place for dinner. I bought my condo a few years ago, as my hangout spot. My place is equipped with a pool table, full bar, a theatre room in the basement, and two king-size bedrooms. April is the first and only person to visit my condo or even know about it. I gave April a spare key when she was going through that tough period in her life with the loss of her baby; I wanted her to know that whatever I had, she was welcomed to it. For dinner that night, I made grilled chicken with Alfredo sauce and penne pasta, homemade garlic biscuits, and I bought her favorite sweet red wine. It was a typical night for us; eat, talk, watch movies and shoot pool. The only difference I noticed that night was the twinkle in April's eyes. It was something I had never seen before; it felt more like an invitation. While we sat on the couch watching movies, April dozed off and I was a little drowsy myself. I woke April up and we decided to go upstairs and shower before we took a nap. April usually left a spare set of clothes at my place but tonight she asked to wear one of my T-shirts. I watched April walk into the bathroom, leaving the door open behind her. The lump in my pants formed from the thought of catching a glimpse of April's naked body.

April turned around and winked at me as I leaned against the bathroom doorway. We never broke eye contact while she teasingly took her hair out of the cute bun style she always wore it in. She pulled her shirt over her head and slowly pulled her tights down and off. She had the body of a goddess; her breasts sat up in her red bra, and she was wearing a matching red thong. My eyes roamed every inch of her body, from the color of her red toe-nail polish, up to the curly hair hanging past her shoulders. April turned around with her back towards me and slowly undid her bra, bent down, touched her toes, and let her thong slide down her thick thighs. I saw every drop of wetness while she bent over; her body was inviting me in. My pants felt too tight from the pressure built up under my jeans. April turned around, licked her sexy lips, and walked into the shower. The gentleman side of me wanted to stand in the corner and watch, but my manly nature took over. I dropped my shirt and pants in one swift move and walked towards the shower. I was nervous as hell and could not believe this was happening, but I was determined to make it all worthwhile.

When I walked into the shower, April stood under the water with her back to me. The water ran down her body, following every curve, creating clear lines down her apple bottom. I couldn't resist any longer, and began kissing the back of her neck and gently licking along the top of her shoulders. The mixture of the water, combined with the natural flavor of her skin, turned me on even more. I leaned in closer to her until my dick stroked the diamond gap under her vagina, between her thighs. April was so wet and slippery that my head slide across her vaginal lips with each rub. I gently turned her around and slowly sucked each breast, making sure to rub my tongue around the sensitive areas of her nipples in a circular motion. Her erect nipples demanded my attention and motivated me to please her even more. April leaned her head back and moaned from my soft kisses. I knelt on one knee and lifted one of her legs to place over my shoulder. She guided her hands to my shoulders to balance herself, and I was now greeting her hot spot before diving in. I used the tip of my tongue to spread them apart with ease, and little by little, licked and tickled her clitoris. Looking up, I stared into her pretty brown eyes, moving my tongue in circular motions around her clit at a consistent pace. I latched my mouth onto her clit licking and sucking until she started grinding her hips into my face. I grabbed and massaged her ass cheeks while she rode my face. Her sweet taste forced me to start stroking my rod with my free hand; the more I stroked, the faster she moved her hips and the deeper my tongue dove into her wetness. April shook from the sensation of her release, and I didn't stop until I heard her moaning my name and begging for me to stop. Leaning against the shower wall for balance, April lifted her leg off my shoulders; I could tell her body was relaxed. Tonight, my only focus was April. I was willing to do whatever I needed to do for her to feel loved and appreciated. I still didn't know what any of this meant for us, and I didn't want to push things any further. After April finished cleaning herself up, she smiled and gave me a long deep kiss before exiting the shower.

I was left experiencing so many different emotions; I thought women were more emotional and were supposed to be the confused ones, but I guess I was wrong. My feelings were stronger for April than I had originally thought. I walked into the dimly lit bedroom; the scent of lavender filled the room from the lit candle. I bought a few candles to keep around the house for April, since she enjoyed lit candles. The stillness in the bedroom confirmed my thoughts that she was sleeping. I eased under the comforter, searching for the warmness of her body with my hands until I touched her bare skin. I moved my hands farther down and felt her soft bottom that I had grown to love, and once again I was aroused. This time, I wasn't going to make any moves unless she wanted me to. As I lay on my side and pulled her body into mine, all I could think about was our future before I quickly dozed off. I didn't know how long I was asleep before the sensation of warm wet liquid running down my penis woke me up. April was under the sheets, taking me entirely in her mouth. The fleshy softness in the back of April's throat brought chills up my spine and made me moan and run my fingers through her hair. My weakness was her excitement; she bobbed her head up and down, faster as she gripped my shaft with her lips and used her tongue to play with the tip of my head in unity. I was in a daze, I wanted to push her away but her mouth felt too good in that moment. I couldn't believe how weak she made my body. April didn't use any hands while balancing my dick and balls in her mouth at the same time and slowly moving her tongue. I couldn't help but admit that April was the first woman to ever bring me to that point of weakness in the bedroom. My toes curled, and I lost all self-control. April stayed steady and consistent; my efforts to pull away from her were worthless. April did not flinch when I released my fluids in her mouth. She licked up and down my shaft, making sure she didn't miss a spot, and left me standing at attention once again. My heart raced as the sweat ran down my chest onto the satin sheets. Before I could recoup, April straddled me and whined her hips slowly. This was the first time I saw the island side of her in motion. Every inch of her body felt so good; her vagina muscles squeezed me and tightened. I relaxed and allowed April to take control slowly, easing down until I was all the way inside of her. I knew I was as deep as I could go when I felt my head hitting her inside walls. She moaned out in pleasure and pain. I grinded my hips into hers, giving her long deep strokes while she rode me. Her juices flowed down my balls and onto the sheets. With each grind, I dove deeper and grabbed her wrist to keep her steady. She kept her hands on my chest until she couldn't balance anymore and lay with her breasts against my chest. With each stroke, her pussy tightened. We continued making love like this all night until we fell asleep from exhaustion.

When I woke up the next morning, April was lying on my chest in a peaceful bliss. Even with her hair in a tangled mess and sleep all over her face, she still was my angel. I exhaled at the thought of what I was about to do and say. But it was time for her to know the truth.

"A...we need to talk." I whispered her nickname, to not startle her out of her sleep.

"Hummm?" April moaned with her eyes halfway opened; she stretched, and then rolled back over.

I was now lying on my side, facing her back. I ran my fingers down the center of her back, observing her natural curves.

"A, please wake up. It's serious."

April rolled over to face me with both her eyes opened. Now that I had her attention, I didn't know what to say or do. I wasn't sure how she would react. April was calm and quiet, which made her unpredictable. However, everyone knew April had a fireball temper, and once she started, no one could stop her. Her anger could go from zero to two hundred in less than a minute. I never quite understood why she became so angry so fast, but I knew her past life had not always been what it seemed to be. I also knew that she loved her sleep; I learned that the hard way on many occasions.

"Okay, I'm up now. You have my full attention…Now stop staring at me like a mad man…what's up?" April yawned.

I didn't mean to stare, but I didn't know how I was going to tell the woman I loved that I was married. *I'm married, I'm married* I repeated that statement in my mind.

"What the fuck did you just say!" April shouted.

April was now sitting up in bed with her back leaning against the headboard. I jumped in shock; I hadn't even realized that the words slipped out of my mouth. April's eyes narrowed in on mine. I froze.

"Christopher Lamar James, *please* tell me that I am hearing things and you didn't say what I just heard?" April's voice was now at an octave-higher level.

I sat up as well, preparing myself to run out of the room if I needed to. I opened my mouth still afraid to speak the words.

"April, you are not hearing things. I …"

WHAP! My face stung. April hit me with so much force, she shook her hand in pain afterwards.

"CJ, if you know what's good for you right now. You won't repeat yourself!" April yelled.

April hardly ever called me CJ; I knew this was serious now. She moved to the edge of the bed and was rocking back and forth with the comforter covering her legs. I didn't know what April was thinking or contemplating on doing next. I was glad she left her purse in the basement last night since that's where she keeps her Beretta. I slowly eased out of the bed to walk to her side of the mattress. I didn't care that I was as naked as a newborn baby. I thought about everything she could do to physically hurt me, but at that point, I deserved that and more. I heard the sniffles and watched her shoulders move up and down. I felt crushed; I knew I had broken her heart. I tried to explain to April that I hadn't had sex with my wife in a year and the government job she had always kept her on the road. When my wife and I have sex, we always use a condom, which explains why we don't have kids. That was one of the many marital problems I was dealing with. The condo we were in right then has always been my getaway spot for years. No one knows about this property except April. I truly needed April to understand that I was in love with her. My marriage felt more like a friendship, but my friendship with April felt more like a marriage. When I was with April, I felt complete. In my heart, I knew that my wife and I would not last forever, but it would take time before we could legally divorce. My wife had invested in my real estate business as well, so I had to tread carefully and make smart decisions. All my pleas to April fell on deaf ears. Her hands covered her eyes as she leaned on her knees.

"You knew so much about me. How could you betray me like this? When did you forget you had a wife? Before or after sex? No, wait! Or did you forget to mention your wife while we had smoothies outside of the gym? So, what did you tell your WIFE when you were by my hospital bed?" April wasn't crying anymore, and her voice was so cold. She repeated the word wife with such disgust and animosity.

I stood in front of her as she spoke. Her mention of the hospital caused tears to fill my eyes, and I didn't stop them from dropping. The pain and hurt April experienced during that moment of her life, I wouldn't wish on my worst enemy. I couldn't believe April thought I would use our friendship as a ploy, like a game I enjoyed playing. I didn't care about all the negative things April said out of anger; all my love was sincere. The only truth I didn't reveal was my wife.

When we first met, April and I were never intimate and were strictly friends, so there had been no need to mention my wife. April didn't ask and I never gave her a reason to ask. I didn't have to hide a wedding ring because I never wore one. Who created the idea of a wedding ring anyway? I always felt that being married began in your heart. A ring does not define your marriage. My wife wanted a ring, so I bought her one. I didn't wear a ring, she understood why, and that was it. Of course, my marriage didn't start the way it was ending, but sometimes people grow apart when they get married for all the wrong reasons, and that is the story of my life. Right then, I needed April to understand that my marriage didn't mean much to me anymore, and she was the woman I needed in my life.

"April, I deeply care for you and our friendship. I don't want that to become something of the past. You're my girl, April. No games needed here. I'm with you and I want you to be with me," I pleaded.

I really needed April to understand my words and feel my honesty. April remained silent, staring into space. I could tell she was thinking of something to say or do, and I didn't expect a response. After everything was revealed, I knew April needed time to digest it all before she made a conscious decision, and I gave her that time. True love is patient. I moved closer to April and she didn't move. I knelt between her legs and moved the comforter to the side. April sat still; lifeless was the best way to describe her stance. I kissed, licked, and massaged her outer thighs until I saw her nipples harden. My face made its way between her legs, and I finished what I had started. I licked and sucked on April until she exploded from pleasure, arched her back, and released the loudest moan I had ever heard.

She relaxed, looked down at me, and said, "I'm leaving."

Crushed, was the best word to describe how I felt at that moment. I watched her get ready to leave.

~

I reflected on my past thoughts of April, which always seemed so current and vivid. I shook my head, placed my cell phone back into the holster on my hip, and prepared for tonight's festivities. I needed to tell April about my pending divorce, but I didn't know when or how I would do it.

THAT MOMENT

"OFTEN TIMES YOUR HEART SEES WHAT IS INVISIBLE TO THE EYE."

riday evening traffic jams seemed to be the worst of the week. I had two hours to get dressed before Chris would be here to pick me up. I took my heels off by the front door and stripped away each piece of clothing while walking through the house. I had a habit of leaving clothes everywhere when I was in a rush, and then I would complain when it was time to clean up. That thought alone forced me to pick up every piece of clothing that I threw all over the house. I was in the process of collecting my discarded clothes when I felt the vibration coming from my purse. I fumbled through lipstick, pens, papers, my Beretta, and everything else before I finally grabbed my cell phone and answered the call.

"Hey, babe!" I said.

"Hey, babe! How was your day?" Ahmad spoke in such a calm manner.

"It was good. I just walked through the door when you called.

I worked longer than normal today, finishing up some things for Jonathan. How was your day? Any new clients?" I asked.

It felt nice and relaxing, listening to Ahmad speak. My anticipation constantly rose each time that we spoke; I couldn't wait to see him in a few weeks. Everything felt so right with Ahmad; he never made it difficult for me to be myself around him. A few days ago, we talked about our future together and our plans of eventually moving in together. I reiterated to Ahmad how serious that decision is to me. I would rather we get married or engaged before I make the decision to move in with him. The amount of time we spent staying overnight at each other's houses did not mean much to me without a ring or a lifelong commitment.

I made myself comfortable on the couch. If I was late, then Chris would have to wait. Ahmad went into detail about his day, and mentioned a new program he wanted to implement into his Community Center in Philadelphia. While Ahmad was playing in the NFL, he bought an old, abandoned, three-story building in the middle of a poverty-stricken neighborhood in Philly. The neighborhood was predominately black with ninety percent of the population in that area consisting of young single mothers. The Community Center provides childcare financial assistance for single parents, including men, raising children alone. The center offered career services for parents, certified drug abuse counselors, and domestic violence programs for battered woman and children. Ahmad wanted to add an educational program to teach African History to African-American youth. He is also opening an outreach center in Birmingham.

I thought about the fact that western culture has brainwashed young children to think that the African- American history taught in primary school is enough. The western education system doesn't teach about the different African tribes or Maroon communities that fought against enslavement. Nor is there any mention of African-American identity or culture. Many history school books don't have pictures of Black leaders. Matter of fact, the only portion of the history book that gives a significant glimpse of Black history is the section that deals with slavery, segregation, and integration. Black history month is not enough time to sculpt young children's minds. Instead, there are so-called reality shows where black women and men are fighting each other like wild animals, often degrading themselves and displaying more hatred and less unity. These television shows teach children less about intelligence and more about beauty or sex appeal. It appears that dark complexion is associated with ugliness, while lighter complexions are associated with beauty. Sex is accepted, while holding out goes unappreciated. The phrases "You are pretty for a dark-skinned girl," or "You have good hair," or "If you're white you're right, if your black get back," are heard all too often in the black community.

How children are raised is a direct reflection of how they treat one another as adults. I could not understand how such a powerful race has such a weak mind. I believe it all stems from the lack of history. If you don't know where you come from, how do you know where you're going? I agreed with Ahmad and believed an African history class for children and parents would benefit the community. Ahmad's knowledge of self and the strength he displays, not only physically but also mentally, makes me fall deeper in love with him. I see a future with Ahmad, and look forward to one day being his wife and carrying his child. The hope of it all excited me even more.

"So, you think the African history class is a good idea?" Ahmad asked, breaking me away from my thoughts.

"Of course. That is a great idea! We need more programs like this for our youth."

I know my opinion matters to Ahmad. There was no need to convince Ahmad of the truth we knew existed. What's understood needs no explanation.

"Thanks, babe. That's why I love you. You always support me in everything I do, and that means more to me than words can explain." Ahmad knew what to say to make my heart melt, even from a distance.

"Awww, Maad, you know I got your back. I have to hold my man down at all times." I blushed.

"I know, and I appreciate that. By the way, before I forget. My mom asked me to remind you to cook curry chicken for her when you come over in a few weeks. You know how she loves your Caribbean meals, especially, my greedy brothers."

We laughed. Ahmad has three brothers who eat like their stomachs are bottom-less pits. Ahmad's family and my family are inseparable. Ahmad only met my mom once but they video chat more often than she calls me.

"Mama A knows that I got her whenever she needs me. I will make enough for everybody, including your greedy self." I smiled.

Ahmad is a food addict, though, fast food or processed food is not his preference. It isn't mine either, but I enjoy my junk food cheat days every now and again, especially when my body craves it.

"Yeah, I know. So, what do you have planned tonight? I'm supposed to hang out with my cousins, but I'm not sure yet about what I want to do." Ahmad yawned.

"I'm hanging out with an old friend. More than likely have a few drinks and shoot pool, nothing major," I said.

Ahmad is a very confident man, so I knew he wouldn't

question much, unless I gave him reasons to do so. He promoted hanging out with friends and having a life outside of our relationship. If it didn't interfere with our relationship, then everything was all good.

"That sounds fun, babe. Well, go ahead and enjoy yourself. I will get off the phone so you can get dressed, since we both know how you like to take your sweet time getting ready. Just call me whenever you can." Ahmad continued laughing as he spoke.

"Whatever, Maad, but I will go ahead and get dressed. I love you and miss you!" I whimpered over the phone.

"I love you and miss you more, babe! Please be safe tonight, okay?" Ahmad pleaded.

"I will, and you do the same. By the way, I got a surprise for you after you hang up the phone. Just a little something to keep your mind occupied tonight." I heard the excitement in Ahmad's voice. He knew exactly what I was about to do.

"Oh yeah? Well, I am hanging up now then! Talk to you later, Queen."

I pulled my panties down to make myself more comfortable on the couch and scrolled to the camcorder application in my cell phone while I lay on the couch with my legs spread open. I placed my cell phone in the holder across from me, pressed record, and put on the best show possible. I made sure I reached an orgasm and that it was captured in the video recording. I sent Ahmad about eight pictures and a full video of me. At least if he decided to stay at home tonight, he would be entertained. After my show, I took a shower and got dressed. I wore a long maxi dress that hugged my hips in all the right places. Cute, simple, and to the point. I dressed exactly how I felt tonight. There was no need for me to impress Chris, but when I step out, I make sure I look good. I moisturized my body and sprayed a little perfume near my intimate areas before I slipped on my ankle sandals. I looked myself over in the mirror once more before I heard my doorbell ring at 9 o' clock sharp. *Chris is always on time,* I thought to myself. I opened my front door and was taken aback for a moment. Chris looked as handsome as ever. By the way his shirt stuck to his arms, it was obvious that he was doubling up on his gym workouts.

"Hey, pretty lady! You ready to go?" Chris said. We hugged; it felt nice to see him.

"I sure am! I only waited forever, slow poke!" I teased.

Our talk during the drive to the bar was far from forceful; we caught up with everything that had happened in our lives over the past six months. Chris learned about Ahmad and our long-distance relationship. He seemed genuinely happy for me. There weren't many silent moments during the drive, but during breaks within our conversation, Chris was in deep thought. It appeared he wanted to tell me something, but he couldn't. I glanced over at him as he drove and noticed how his eyebrows creased in the middle, visibly reasoning with himself.

I had such an exciting time at the bar with Chris. We played a few rounds of pool. Between the drinks and shooting pool, I had a nice buzz. Other people joined in and created pool teams. After a few hours at the bar, Chris invited me to his place to hang out and watch a movie. I didn't mind, considering we have not hung out in over six months. I had a few more drinks at his place while we relaxed and watched comedy movies in his theatre room. I kept stretching my neck and back, I was sore all week from gym work-outs. I made a mental note to schedule an appointment at the spa as soon as possible. Chris must have read my mind.

"Hey, you've been stretching all night like an old woman! Let me give you a massage."

His statement was more of a request. The drinks I had consumed all night were finally catching up with me. I felt relaxed, woozy, and a little drowsy.

"Well, I guess so, since I am looking like an old woman, as you say it. I might just need a massage. I hope you don't scratch my back with those dry hands." We laughed at my comment as I stretched out along his couch.

Chris unbuckled my sandals and massaged my feet. The sensation of his touch sent a tingling feeling throughout my body that rested between my legs. I was too relaxed to move. Chris slowly moved his hands up and down my legs, massaging all my pressure points. The soft fabric of my dress, combined with the strength of his hands against my skin, felt amazing. I quickly dozed off but was awakened by wet kisses up and down my thighs and around my bottom. My wetness ran down my thighs and soaked his leather sofa. Chris slowly ran his tongue up and down the insides of the back of my thighs, while tenderly rolling me over to remove my dress and massage the front of my body. His mouth felt warm. I hadn't realized how much my body missed him until this moment. My mind told me to get off the couch and stop him, but my heart and body were of one accord, and I couldn't move. I wasn't sure if I was still feeling the effects of the alcohol or if it was something more. The heat of this intense moment caused my nipples to poke out like budding flowers. He made his way on top of me, kissing my neck and licking my breasts. With every move, he slowly and carefully unlocked each area of my body. I felt him slide inside of me; each deep stroke sent my mind into a passionate bliss. I wrapped my legs around his waist, digging my nails deeper into his back. I couldn't hate Chris, no matter how hard I tried. My mind swirled as our skin collided. I couldn't ignore the fact that I felt my body yearning for his love and affection; it was like a monster that was finally getting fed. The tighter I wrapped my legs, the deeper his thrust. My back tightened as my walls squeezed his dick. I could not control my shaking thighs or the fire I felt on the inside as we released at the same time. I exhaled before I dozed off again. In that moment, I finally understood the meaning of the statement, *the sweetest sin*.

The next morning, I awoke to the smell of bacon. This was odd because no one has keys to my house except Kesha, and I know Kesha isn't over here cooking. I opened my eyes, sat up, yawned, and looked around. I almost fell out of the bed when I realized where I was. Before I could gather my thoughts or my emotions, Chris walked into the room, carrying a plate of food with a glass of orange juice on a tray. Chris placed the tray on the dresser.

"Rise and shine, sunshine!" Chris said with the brightest smile on his face.

I quickly stood up, but almost lost my balance from dizziness. I held my hand to my head in disbelief that I was at Chris's house and had awakened in his bed, wearing his shirt with no panties on.

"Whoa, whoa, take it easy now. We drank way too much last night, and you drank a little more than usual." Chris held out his arms, prepared to catch me if I fell. I knew he was nervous because he couldn't read my thoughts. I remained silent, trying to piece together last night's events. Chris walked towards me with two ibuprofen pills in his hand and pointed to the glass of water on the nightstand next to me.

"Here, take this for the headache, April. You should feel better very soon. Just try to relax."

I threw my head back and gulped the water and pills down.

Last night's festivities rushed to my mind at once. I had a flashback of Chris on top of me and the pleasure I'd felt last night.

"No, no, no!" I stood up with my hands covering my face as I thought about Ahmad. The guilt was unbearable.

"How could I be so stupid! How could you let me be so stupid?" I repeated those questions out loud, knowing Chris didn't have an answer for me, just as I didn't have an answer for myself. The questions were more for me than Chris. Chris stood speechless, holding his head down in shame.

"April, please don't think I took advantage of you. I would never do such a thing. We both were wrapped up in the moment. I know I should have controlled myself, but I couldn't resist... You just have a hold on me. I deeply apologize for not being the bigger person. I'm sorry."

I considered Chris's pleading eyes and immediately felt remorseful, but my guilt was overbearing. I flashbacked to the intense pleasure I felt last night and became aroused, but I would never admit that to Chris. I sat in silence, not knowing what to say next.

"Please, say something. I hope this doesn't end our friendship. There's so much we can still learn about each other. I would like to talk to you about something very important. But since you're not saying anything, I won't push it. I will take you home as soon as you finish eating."

Chris started to walk out of the room with his head down, clearly defeated. I decided to speak before he walked out of the room.

"It's okay, Chris. You've done enough for me. Just know that this will never happen again. I am in a happy place, and I have to move forward with my life."

Chris turned around and listened as I spoke. I sensed his hurt, but I hurt too. The truth doesn't always feel good, but I needed to face the music, and so did he. I ate in silence as my mind flooded with thoughts of everything.

I deeply love and care about Chris and truly respect our friendship. I know, if he weren't married we would have been together but I also know he would never leave his wife. I never received the full back story about his marital situation and right now I don't care to know. I was happy with Ahmad, I felt I belonged with Ahmad, it is my destiny. I am disappointed in myself about the events that took place last night, but more saddened because I know this is the end of a friendship that was cultivated for years. He needs to move on with his wife and I need to move on with my life.

HANGOVER

"SOMETIMES THE STRONGEST THING YOU CAN DO IS LEAVE…"

The taxi ride home was uncomfortable, but I'd rather ride with a stranger than deal with the awkward silence between Chris and I. I walked into my house, took off my sandals, threw my purse on the couch, and didn't bother checking my cell phone. I needed to sit in silence for a moment and get my mind in order. I felt confused, hurt, angry, and disgusted all at once. As I tried to relax, my house phone rang. Very few people have my house phone number, so I knew it had to be an important call.

"Hello?" I didn't mask my groggy voice.

"Dang! Did you just wake up or something?" Kesha knew exactly how to aggravate me.

"Well, if I was trying to sleep, you weren't going to let that happen, were you?" I yawned in between my statement.

"I sure wasn't! I hardly see or speak with you during the week. I guess Ahmad got your legs and arms tied up." Kesha laughed, tickling herself, I guess.

"Girl, I guess. You are right. I am always busy during the week, if I am not at hubby's house. Anyway, I should be in Alabama in a few weeks."

I stood up to undress; I needed to blow off some steam at the gym.

"Oh, la la! Sounds to me like I need to start planning a wedding. I think I hear wedding bells. You and Ahmad have gotten so close in these past few months. I'm so happy for you," Kesha exclaimed.

"A wedding? I wouldn't say all of that. But, I do believe in speaking it into existence."

I placed Kesha's call on the speaker phone while I got up and put on my gym clothes.

"All I can say is, I hope so. You deserve to be happy." Kesha constantly spoke those words to me.

"Who said I'm not happy? Do I need a man to make me happy?" I asked.

I often wondered why some women associated happiness with relationships. Of course, I absolutely love being with Ahmad, but my personal happiness does not rely on Ahmad. He contributes to my joy, does not take it away, and I make sure I do the same for him. No one should ever want to be in an unfulfilling relationship. Committing to a needy or jealous person is a recipe for disaster. I learned from experience, that I choose not to repeat.

"Come on, A, you know I didn't mean it like that. I mean it as, sometimes you feel more whole as a woman when you're with a man. Not just any man, but a good man who is all yours. Ain't nothing like it!"

It's easy for Kesha to say that. She has been with Rob for almost five years. They both have had their ups and downs, but never gave up on each other. I keep telling her to have babies, but she is adamant on waiting until marriage. I don't believe a marriage certificate decides a man's faithfulness, but every woman, obviously, doesn't feel the same way. My belief is that every man cheats at some point; most grow out of it and determine to remain faithful, while others never change, for one reason or another. I would hate to think that my man is unfaithful but in my current situation, I have no room to judge.

"I agree with you. I love Ahmad, and it does feel good to me, knowing that I have a strong man to depend on. I miss him a lot when we aren't around each other. I don't know how much longer I can deal with the distance." I fondled with my shoe laces.

I grabbed my car keys and walked out the front door. I connected my phone to the Bluetooth in my car as we continued in conversation.

"All I can say is true love is patient. If your relationship can survive through long distance, then it will make you both stronger. Ahmad loves you, April, and I am so happy for the both of you."

Kesha's words warmed my heart; it is always nice to have a supportive friend.

"Thanks, Kesh! That means a lot to me. Let me head to the gym before you get me all emotional and stuff!"

"Cool, we'll chat later. Work out for me and you!" Kesha said.

We hung up, and then I dialed my future husband's number. The phone ring-back tone played through my car speakers. *All of me,* John Legend sang those words so perfectly. I smiled, listening to the ring tone Ahmad had assigned specifically for me.

"Hey, babe." It was evident that he was lying down by the sound of his voice. I was relieved to hear his voice.

"Hey, love! What's up with you?" I said.

"Nothing much. Just left the gym and lying across the couch, relaxing for a second. You must have had a fun time last night since I haven't heard from you, not even a text." I could sense Ahmad's curiosity through his words. I made up my mind to leave last night's events in the past and never speak about what happened.

"I apologize about that. I had a good time last night, woke up with a hangover. You know how I do!" I smiled.

"Yeah, I know how *you* do, but I'm glad you enjoyed yourself. Next time, shoot me a text or something because I was a little worried. You know I get nervous when I don't hear from my lady. These streets aren't safe. I can't wait to see you," Ahmad said.

"Me too! That is all I keep thinking about. I'm on my way to the gym now to make sure I'm nice and tight for my superman," I teased.

"Oh yeah! That's what I'm talking about. My lady always keeps herself up. That's what I love about you," Ahmad said.

I love it when he calls me his lady.

"And you know this! I'm pulling into the gym parking lot now, hubby. I will call you when I finish my workout."

"No problem. I love you."

I never grew tired of hearing those words out of his mouth.

"I love you too, Maad." The resonated sound of *call ended,* echoed through my car speakers as I exited my car for the gym.

KESHA

*T*he conversation I had with April remained on my mind as I drove home from the grocery store. I thought about April's current relationship. Through all the years I've known April, I have witnessed her transformation into a beautiful woman. I was also by her side throughout the heartbreak that she experienced. Often, I wondered if April would ever get a break, and many times I ran out of words to encourage her. April truly is a good person, inside and out, but for some reason, bad situations always find her. April remained single ever since RJ was born, and I tried to hook her up on dates plenty of times, which resulted in failure. So, when April clicked with Ahmad, it was a breath of fresh air for me. They are such a beautiful couple, and I can't wait to surprise April in a few weeks.

I was so deep in thought that the drive home seemed quicker than normal. Rob met me at the front door before I could stick my key in the doorknob. He greeted me with a kiss, then took the grocery bags out my hand and unpacked the groceries in the kitchen.

"So, how has your day been?" Rob said.

I watched his muscular arms reach into the cabinet to place a bag of brown rice. He normally only wore gym shorts in the house, unless we had company over. Staring at his chest caused my nipples to harden.

"I actually had a good day today. Woke up next to my man and made it back home safely, greeted by my man. What more can I ask for? Aside from that, I spoke to April earlier, and she has no clue about what's going to happen in a few weeks. All she talks about is how bad she wants to see Ahmad."

I took my hair out of the ponytail, sat back in the recliner, and relaxed.

"That's great news! I can't wait to see the expression on her face. It's going to be priceless. As a matter of fact, there is something that has been on my mind that I want to talk to you about," Rob said.

Rob leaned his back against the counter, staring at me. I gazed at his chiseled chest, and the last thing I wanted to do was talk.

"I'm all ears, baby. What's up?" I licked my lips.

"Kesha, I'm ready for us to start a family. We are both set in our careers. Well, I am, since you don't have to work unless you want to. I'm ready, but I want to know how you feel about it since you would be the one carrying her for nine months."

Rob was right. It is time for us to start a family. When we moved in together four years ago, I worked as a nurse practitioner part-time while attending a master's degree program full-time. My aspiration is to one day own a pediatric clinic. A few years ago, Rob's construction business was starting up, so money and time were not on our side in the beginning. It was rough on our relationship; the pressure and stress almost ended our relationship, but we stayed down. I wasn't on birth control, and we weren't using condoms, but often I would make him pull out during sex for fear of getting pregnant. I would never forget the day when I was sitting next to April's hospital bed and I saw the pictures she sent me after she gave birth. I cried when I saw those pictures, but I could never cry in front of her. The thought of being in that situation scared me, but I didn't want to live my life in fear. I know Rob is ready and so am I, but I am uncomfortable with the idea that we aren't married yet.

"Well, I have been giving it some thought as well, and I am ready to start a family, but you know how I feel about marriage. I want us to be married first, and how do you know our first is going to be a girl anyway?"

"Come on, Kesha, you know I'm not going anywhere. I've been saving money to make sure you can have the wedding of your dreams. We can start planning now for a wedding. It's all about what you want. I just know our first baby will be a beautiful girl, trust me." Rob smiled.

I knew Rob wasn't going anywhere, especially after he placed this big rock on my finger, but I felt that a marriage certificate made it difficult for both parties to leave.

"*Yeah, right!* Don't tell me I can plan now and then change your mind later." I rolled my eyes at him, leaning back into the recliner.

"Change my mind! You're joking, right? You think I would invest years into our relationship to change my mind? You stayed down with me when I barely had shit, and now we don't even have to think twice when it comes to spending money. I created this lifestyle so you don't have to work. I don't want you to work unless you want to. So, when I tell you I am ready, please don't second guess my feelings for you and us. Baby, I'm in this for the long haul, so let's make it happen."

The sternness in Robert's voice showed me how serious he was. I didn't intend for my comment to offend him. His eyes narrowed in on mine, most likely he was trying to read my mind. I slowly stood up from the recliner and walked over to Rob pretending I was upset. When I was within arm's reach, I jumped into his arms with my legs wrapped around him and passionately kissed him. I licked his earlobe, and I whispered in his ear.

"I'm ready to make it official. Now let's start planning the wedding and making our baby."

Lust dripped off every word I spoke as the words rolled off my tongue. Rob carried me into the kitchen, laid me across the kitchen counter, unzipped, pulled down my pants, and spread my legs. I tilted my head back as he worked his tongue magic. We made love for the next few hours and into the night.

AHMAD

*E*verything is prepared and ready to go for my big day in a few weeks. I pray it runs perfectly. April's mom's flight lands during the week, and she will be staying with my mom. I made all the phone calls and invited everyone that I wanted to be there. Now all I needed to do was wait and watch it all unfold. April didn't know her life was about to change for the better very soon. My thoughts were interrupted by my phone ringing.

"Hello?"

"Hey, Maad! I just left the gym. On my way home. I had a great workout. What are you up to?"

April sounded happy, as she usually did when she worked out. "I'm sure you did. Got those buns firm and juicy for daddy, huh?" Just the thought of April's body aroused me.

"You know how I do. I did a few extra squats just for you."

"I like the sound of that. My lady gets it in at the gym!" I smiled.

Since I met April, our greatest attraction to each other has been how in touch we are with our bodies. After I stopped playing football, I quickly learned how important it is to take care of your body. I maintained my weight during football season because of my defensive position, but after I stopped playing football, there was no need to remain as heavy as I was. I also wasn't eating very healthy while I played in the NFL. It took a lot of discipline and time for me to adjust to healthier lifestyle habits, especially after I learned that diabetes and high blood pressure are prevalent in the black community. I didn't want to become another statistic, so I changed my eating habits.

"I feel more relaxed now," April said. "Just need to take a hot shower and chill out today. I have been calling Kesha all afternoon to try to catch up with her, but she won't answer her phone. Guess she must be having a long day. Anyway, I'm going to go home, clean up, and pack so I'll be ready to come see you," April said.

"Babe, you sure are a germaphobe. You are the only person I know who lives alone and cleans the house every two or three days, as if you have ten kids. I can't believe you're packing now for three weeks out!" Ahmad joked.

I enjoyed talking to April, and never grew tired of our conversations. We talked on the phone the rest of the afternoon and video chatted before we went to sleep. Plenty of times, we fell asleep while video chatting online, and I'd wake up in the middle of the night only to see her sleeping peacefully through the computer screen. April has a loving heart but was taken advantage of by all the wrong men. I will never hurt April like those other guys did, but she will see how serious I am very soon. I'm ready to spend the rest of my life with April; I want to give her the love she deserves.

LIVING MY LIFE LIKE IT'S GOLDEN

"SECOND CHANCES ARE BETTER THAN
NONE AT ALL."

*A*ll I thought about was seeing Ahmad while I listened to Jill Scott booming through my speakers and drove toward Ahmad's house. I continued singing along with Jill Scott, *living my life like it's golden.* I was moving my head as though I were performing on stage. No wonder other drivers were smiling and honking their horns as they rode past me. But I didn't care; I was on a natural high. The next song that played was India Aire's, *God Is Real.* That song brought many emotions of gratitude out of me but often made me wonder. When I was younger, I grew accustomed to attending church every Sunday and witnessing the same people who prayed and praised next to me, curse somebody out as soon as church was over. I wondered how religion was followed during slavery and segregation days. Black folks and white folks supposedly prayed to the same God, but black folks were treated worse than dirt because of their skin color. How could a pastor agree with inhumane treat because of skin color? How could one pray to God or Jesus, but whip another human being so badly, that the flesh ripped off their skin like a blown-out tire? Why did God allow Africans to remain enslaved for so long and be treated as property? I pondered these questions for years. It took a lot of research and soul searching for me to find peace within myself.

Growing up in the black community, I was raised to never question God. So, as my curiosity grew, so did my research. I learned that when Africans were brought to America, they were feared by many whites (Europeans, British) because the Africans fought back, especially the men. The Africans also leaned on their spiritual rituals for strength. When the slave masters realized that the Africans would not conform, and recognized that their strength lay in the African men, they began removing the bonds that kept the tribes together. The enslaved African men were warriors and were determined to protect their tribes.

To break this disobedience, the slave masters castrated the African men in front of others and implemented fear that spread throughout the plantation. The African women feared the white men so much that they began to lose faith and trust in their African men. The white men also realized that the Africans' strength came from rituals and praying, so the slave owners decided to teach the good obedient slaves, mainly women, the English language, and introduce them to westernized Christian religion. This method spread like wildfire, and within years, many slaves learned how to read and felt obligated to obey what was written in the Bible regarding slavery and disobedience. This was why many slaves remained in their condition, for fear of disobeying God and their slave masters. The Bible does mention for "slaves to obey their masters," so why would they run? Why would they disobey? I understand that each book in the Bible was written by different authors. Each chapter was written to suit the time and person writing it. When my eyes were opened to the truth, I was in disbelief and confused. It was a lot of unfamiliar information to digest that went against everything I had been raised to believe. God cannot be fit into a box; there is way more to the Holy Bible than the human eye can see. Much of the African's ancestral knowledge is lost or hidden.

Once my spiritual eye was opened, I realized the true extent of the damage done. Many questions flooded my mind, like why black churches have pictures of a white Jesus or why many blacks fought for integration to have business alongside their white counterparts, only to lose their own businesses in the process. I now understood why other races owned the supermarkets or corner stores within the black community, especially the beauty supply stores. While in the process of supporting other businesses, black folks lost their own.

The truth saddens me, but I refuse to fall into that category, which is why I own my business. If I am blessed to have children, I will raise all of them to be entrepreneurs. I once heard a quote, "The religion you believe is based on the principles you choose to follow." That statement is very true, which is my philosophy. I know God is real and my life is not by chance. I try to continuously live right and not go against my morals and values. My relationship with the Most High is through prayer, meditation, and sacrifice, and I truly believe that Karma always prevails. In the end, love has no face or shape, it is an action.

I was deep in thought, and I almost passed my exit on the highway. I looked up and noticed my exit was less than a half-mile away. I am staying with Ahmad for two weeks. I desperately needed this break. I wanted to visit him sooner but he persisted that I arrive on Wednesday. It was unusual for Maad to want me in town during the middle of the week, but I agreed.

I thought about Chris every now and then and wondered if he was okay, but I ignored his calls on purpose. Sometimes it is best to think about someone rather than speak to that person. As much as I sincerely cared about Chris, I had to get him out of my system.

As I approached Ahmad's house, I envisioned living in Ahmad's neighborhood. The thought of us having a family brought joy to my heart. When I pulled into his driveway, Maad was waiting at the front door, holding a bushel of assorted colored tulips in a red vase. He always had great timing and knew exactly when I would arrive. I took my shades off, used my hand to flatten the wild strands of my hair, reapplied lip gloss, and stepped out of the car. I didn't have a chance to close the car door before Ahmad scooped me into his arms. I felt like a rag doll. My five-foot-nine-inch, and 160-pound frame was like a mouse being captured by a lion. All I could do was succumb to his hold and relax in his arms. He used his body as pressure to hold me against the car as he gently and passionately kissed me. Strands of my stubborn hair fell back down and lay between our lips intuitively to block our kisses. We pulled away at the same time and laughed as I kept trying to blow my hair away from my mouth.

I walked into the house and relaxed while Ahmad got my bags out of the trunk. The fresh lavender scent greeted me; I was not surprised that the house is in the same condition since I was last here. Ahmad's house is beautiful, with a modern look, but it was lacking that feminine touch to make it a home. On my last visit, I bought a few wall paintings and several types of pottery that I placed in different areas of the house. The little that I did made an enormous difference in the home décor. Upon entering the living room, I saw a huge painting of an African family, a mother breastfeeding her baby while the father held the baby to her chest. That picture alone created a cozy environment and convinced me to lie across the suede loveseat and rest. I felt a warm kiss on my forehead and I opened my eyes to see Ahmad standing over me, smiling.

"Babe, you had been asleep for a while. I was afraid you would miss dinner so I had to wake you up."

I sat up and held my head. The lights were on in the living room, and I didn't see any sunlight outside through the living room window. These past few weeks have been stressful, but I didn't realize the stress had taken such a toll on my body. I also felt nauseous. I thought about the fast food I ate for breakfast that morning and shook my head. Fast food for breakfast is never a good idea for me. I stood up, yawned, and stretched my arms.

"Wow! I didn't realize I fell asleep. I wasn't drowsy, but I guess it crept up on me," I said. Even after my nap, my body remained sore from fatigue.

"Yeah, you slept pretty long. I already have a bubble bath set for you. Just go upstairs, relax, and soak. Dinner should be ready by the time you're finished."

I couldn't help but smile as I stared into Ahmad's eyes. I love him for always looking out for me. There aren't many men who will take the lead in the relationship without the woman asking. These characteristics are what attracted me to Ahmad; his considerate personality makes me fall deeper in love with him every day.

"Thank you, hubby! Every day I am falling deeper in love with you. Pretty soon you're not going to be able to get rid of me," I said.

"That's what I like to hear." He winked.

We shared a wet kiss. Maad slapped my ass as I walked past him, going up the stairs to the bathroom. Before I got in the water, I looked at my body in the mirror, observing every defect that makes me unique. I slowly dipped my body into the warm, steaming water that swallowed every inch of my skin. I felt the water touch my earlobes. I heard the soft soap suds pop as my eyes closed. My muscles relaxed and my mind drifted off to another place. All I needed then was a glass of wine to set the tone. I smiled when I noticed the bottle of wine inside of the ice bucket, next to the hot tub. I don't know how I managed to miss that. Guess I was more focused on getting into the hot tub. I poured a glass of red wine and did a few neck rotations before I took a sip. My body was sore from the drive and from working out this past week. The sweet taste of the wine excited my taste buds. Unfortunately, my stomach did not agree with my mouth. After a few sips, I felt knots forming in my stomach as my mouth salivated. Suddenly, the smell and taste of the wine didn't seem so pleasurable. The knots in my stomach turned into a mixture of fluids. My stomach felt like a blender with different liquids brewing around. I jumped out of the water and barely made it to the toilet before everything flowed out of my mouth and into the toilet bowl. I have not had a stomach virus in a very long time; this was not the time or place for the occasion.

I regained my composure, drained the tub water, and walked over to the shower. I loved how Ahmad's bathroom was so spacious, but walking around his bathroom was more of a burden than a blessing in this moment. I stepped into the shower while the hot water beat on my skin; I traced the water with my eyes as it ran down my skin. It reminded me of water running down a brown tree limb. I was more upset than anything else that I couldn't enjoy my wine. I made a mental note to never eat at that hole- in- the wall fast-food joint again, that I had stopped at on the way to Alabama. I felt even more drained after I finished my shower. If these symptoms didn't subside in a few days, I would have to find a doctor in the area. I dried off with the red towel on the towel rack. Red is our favorite color so Ahmad normally coordinated his home décor with that color. I pinned my wet hair up in a bun, put on my black satin gown, and walked downstairs. The smell of hot dinner permeated the walls and stimulated my senses, causing my stomach to grumble. Ahmad set dinner on the table and poured a glass of his famous fruit smoothie for me to drink.

"Here, this will make you feel better. I heard you praying at the toilet upstairs," Ahmad said while laughing.

I couldn't help but smile and slap his arm. I drank the smoothie, and my stomach automatically calmed down. Within a few moments, I was back to normal, with a big appetite. Ahmad cooked baked fish, yellow rice, and fresh broccoli. It was a nice healthy dinner, and most importantly, it stayed down. We usually take turns washing dishes, but I was too exhausted to do anything other than sleep.

"The dinner was delicious, hubby, and that smoothie made my stomach feel so much better. Now it's time for us to relax. I'll clean the kitchen tomorrow, babe. Let's go to bed." My eyes were watery from yawning.

"Okay, love. I wanted to clean the kitchen tonight, but since you insist, I guess it can wait until tomorrow."

Ahmad grabbed my hand as I followed him upstairs to the bedroom. My man always leads me, even in the household. I took off my gown and lay under the comforter, naked. Ahmad did the same; this was a normal routine for us. I cuddled under Ahmad's arms and fell asleep. As we lay there, I realized this was exactly where I wanted to be.

OUR LOVE

"LOVE IS A POWERFUL DRUG, CONTROL THE ADDICTION OR LOSE CONTROL ...YOUR CHOICE."

The sunlight escaped through the curtains and landed on my eyelids. My eyelids twitched from trying to remain closed. I rolled over into Ahmad's arms and kissed his neck.

"Good morning, Queen." Ahmad's eyes were shut as he spoke.

"Now, how did you know my eyes were opened?" I cleared my throat to get rid of the grogginess.

"You know I know a little bit of everything, Queen. I know when you're awake. You want everyone else to be awake."

Ahmad opened his eyes, rolled over on top of me, and smiled. Even with sleepiness on his face, his handsomeness sent volts through my heart. I leaned my face forward and kissed him. You know you truly love someone when you can kiss them with morning breath. In the middle of our kiss, Ahmad's phone vibrated. For the past few months, every now and then, his phone would ring or vibrate, and he would look at the caller ID and never answer. I observed all of this, but realized in due time if he was hiding something, the truth would reveal itself.

"So, tonight, I want to take you somewhere special. I want you to put on a nice dress but make sure you're comfortable," Ahmad said.

"You know I don't like surprises, Maad, so at least give me a clue."

I gently rubbed my finger down the back of his neck; I knew he would like the feeling.

"That feels good, babe, but you know I still can't tell you *everything*, but I can tell you that we will be at a nice restaurant."

If anybody knew at least one thing about me, it would be that I love food, especially seafood.

"Okay, I'll take that! Now I'm excited!" I hugged him as tight as I could while he lay on top of me. I felt his manhood grow as I pulled him closer to my body. The pressure from his weight on top of me squeezed my chest. My juice box pulsated at the thought of him inside of me. I spread my legs from under his body and wrapped my legs around his waist. He slid inside of me with ease, making sure his long strokes hit every area of my insides. Ahmad always found G-spots inside of me that I didn't even know existed. My nipples stiffened and my walls tightened with each stroke he delivered. Ahmad sucked and licked on my nipples until my nipples looked like little Soldiers standing at attention, waiting for the next command. The sensation of his tongue on my breast, combined with his fullness inside of me, sent my body into overdrive. I tightened my legs around his waist and continued moaning his name until I couldn't take the pleasure anymore. My knees buckled and my back muscles tightened as all my juices flowed off his thick rod and onto the satin sheets. Before I could regain my composure, Ahmad sped up his pace and, with one motion, flipped me over as he held my hands behind my back. I bit the pillow, spread my hips, and tooted my ass up as high as it could go to allow him deeper access. The sensation of his balls slapping against my pussy lips and the sweat running down my breasts onto the sheets turned me on even more. I tried blowing my hair out of my face as I was about to reach another climax. Ahmad squeezed both my ass cheeks and pushed his hip into me even harder as we moaned and released together. Ahmad collapsed on top of my back and kissed the back of my neck. The thoughts of my surprise tonight caused me to smile before we dozed off from our lovemaking.

MY QUEEN

"NURTURER, LOVER, WARRIOR...TRUST IN ME TO UPLIFT YOU."

I admired April's body as she stood in front of me, teasing me with her hips. I loved every inch of her body, from the loose strands of hair hanging across her face, down to the scar on her hip that remained hidden. A few years ago, April noticed a discolored pigmentation mark on her skin. Her doctor cut a nice size area of skin off her hip to test it for cancerous cells. Unfortunately, that area never healed properly, and April was very self-conscious about that area of her body. With each intimate moment, I made it my duty to always rub or kiss that area; all of April's impurities and insecurities were perfect to me. From her perky breasts to her long strong legs that I enjoyed wrapped around my body. For such a small framed woman, her body was proportionate and her ass had just the right amount of firmness to it. April bent over, picked her panties up off the floor, and looked back at me seductively. As I stood up to walk towards her, she closed the bathroom door. I shook my head; this woman enjoyed teasing me. I sat on the bed and noticed my phone blinking; I touched the screen, five missed calls and three text messages. I cringed when I recognized the first two missed calls from a familiar number I'd been avoiding; the others were from April's mom and Rob. I held the phone to my ear with my shoulder while it rang.

"Well, hello there! I thought you would never call me back!"

April's mom spoke in excitement. I overheard my mom's voice in the background.

"Of course, I was going to call you back, Ma. I can't do it while April is around though." I smirked.

Everyone called April's mother Ma. She was one of those women who took everyone under her wing. She lived by the quote, "It takes a village to raise a child."

"Where is she now? Are you ready for your big night?" Ma said.

"She is in the shower. I am beyond ready, Ma. I knew this day would come early on in our relationship, and I don't want to ever lose her." I was ready, and relieved that everything was finally falling into place.

"Ahmad, mi soon cry! Jah kno! Mi happy fi mi daughta! Mi can't wait to see deh expression pon er face!" Ma's excitement brought a smile to my face.

"I know, Ma. I can't wait either. Remember, my family is not from Jamaica, so when you get excited, you have to slow down while you're speaking so everyone can understand you."

"Aye, look here. Don't try me like I don't know how to speak proper English! Okay?" I laughed even harder as I listened to Ma try to straighten me over the phone.

"Yes, Ma, I know. Tell my mom I said hello. I hear her laughing in the background. I just heard the water stop in the shower. Let me get off the phone before April suspects something," I whispered for fear that April may have overheard the conversation.

"You're right. We don't want to ruin the surprise. We love y 'all and see you soon," my mom and April's mom spoke in unison. Those women are a trip when they are together. I hung up and texted Rob to confirm that everything was on point on his end.

Me: What's good Rob?

Rob: You tell me bro! You ready for your big day?

Me: You all crack me up with this big day thing! Yes, I am ready for tonight. I know she is the one.

Rob: Ha! That's what they all say, but I'm just joking. I am happy for you bro! I know you'll do the right thing and April is a good woman.

Me: Thanks man that means a lot coming from you. I'm tryna get like you and Kesha.

Y 'all are like Bonnie and Clyde over there building empires.

Rob: LOL! Yeah but Rome wasn't built in a night, and trust me, we have put in major work to get this far but I don't see it no other way.

Me: That's what's up! How is the wedding planning going?

Rob: It's going good. To be honest, man I have no idea. I just sit around and let Kesha do her thing as I watch my bank account dwindle away. As long as she is smiling, then that's a good thing.

Me: LMBO! Come on bro! You gotta be more involved than that!

Rob: Aye, look man. You'll see when y 'all start planning your wedding. These women put on an entirely different hat, and push you out the picture while they plan. That makes it easier for me; Lord knows wedding planning is not something men are all excited about. I'll be more excited when I watch her walk down the aisle towards me.

Me: I feel you on that! Well, April is out the shower and giving me that look, so I'll see y 'all later.

Rob: All right bro, see ya soon! Think I just heard the whip sound! ☺

Me: LOL! Whatever man. See ya later.

~

*I*t was almost noon, and the weather was sunny and beautiful outside. April and I decided to have lunch at a nearby park. The park was unusually packed for a weekday. I watched a group of women power walking while pushing baby strollers with their earphones on. I didn't understand the point of walking with a baby club if everyone had earphones on. I thought the purpose was to mingle and talk with each other while walking. It didn't make any sense to me, but a lot of what women do don't make any sense to me, but I guess that's what makes me a man. April concentrated, reading through pages in a magazine she held. I watched as she pushed her glasses up on her nose every few minutes to prevent them from falling off her face. I decided against interrupting her thoughts. I was so focused on April's facial expression that I didn't see the soccer ball roll across the field towards us. I looked down at a colorful soccer ball next to my shoe, trying to figure out where it came from. I grabbed the ball and looked up to notice a little boy, not more than four years old, running towards me. Just watching the cute little boy run towards me in his colorful shirt and light up shoes made me want my own family even more. His thick Afro and funny run caused me to smile. I handed the ball out for him.

"Thank you, Sir!" The boy grabbed the ball out of my hand and ran over to his dad, who waved at me. I waved back and continued my observation around the park. April still hadn't lifted her face from out of the magazine.

"That must be a good read, huh? My lady not showing her man no love."

"Oh, stop it! I was just reading an article about a few planned construction buildings around this way. It would actually be a nice location for my business," April said.

"So, you're saying that you are going to move here?" My eyebrows lifted with surprise and suspense at the same time.

"Well, if you must know. I am thinking about it. That's all." April tried to make it seem like it was more of a thought than a plan, but I saw right through her facade.

"Uh huh! So, you say. Honestly, I would love for you to be here with me. We've been apart long enough," I said.

"I agree, babe. I love you." April grabbed my hand and kissed it.

"I love you too. More than words can express." I placed my arm over her shoulders and watched as the crowd grew at the park. We had about four hours left before we needed to be at the restaurant tonight. I know April needs at least two hours to get ready, so it was time to leave the park.

"The park is getting more crowded and I don't want us to be late for our dinner reservations. Are you ready to go yet?"

"Yes, you know I need time to get ready," April winked.

I'm glad we left when we did because traffic downtown was a beast. While April took her time getting dressed, I used that moment to send a mass text message to everyone, confirming tonight's reservations. I decided to wait downstairs for April until she had finished getting dressed. When I saw her walking downstairs, I stood in amazement. April wore a long black dress that stuck to every curve on her body like a glove. April's natural beauty didn't require much make-up or jewelry to stand out. While most women had to speak loud or wear revealing clothing to get attention, April didn't need to do any of that. Her demeanor and uniqueness demanded the attention she desired. As I matured, I stopped looking at women who wore fewer clothes and spoke the most. I found myself attracted to women who didn't force their minds or bodies on men. That's what I loved about April. She is confident in her own skin; there is nothing more attractive than a confident woman.

"Why are you staring at me like that?" April flashed that smile I love as she spoke.

"Why can't I? My lady is beautiful! You smell good too. I am going to keep you close tonight." I winked at her with a smirk on my face.

"Thanks, babe! You always look so handsome, and you don't have to keep me close because I am already here." We kissed and made our way out of the door.

APRIL

*A*hmad looks so handsome tonight in his crème linen suit and cream alligator skin loafers to match. His long, groomed locs extended past his broad shoulders, giving him a strong exotic look. I loved everything about this man, from his alluring eyes down to his strong hands. Every inch of his body spoke volumes to mine, and I planned on showing him tonight everything I felt. Ahmad held my hand on the drive to the restaurant; his hands felt warm and moist, as though he was nervous. I truly hope this man is not bringing me to a nice restaurant to reveal a devastating secret to me. The thought of it all made my heart feel like it was going to beat out of my chest.

When we pulled up to the restaurant, Ahmad stepped out and spoke a few words to the valet before he handed over his car keys. Ahmad opened my door and held my hand as I stepped out of the car in my five-inch stilettos. I was in awe as we walked into the restaurant. The employees were very friendly, and the atmosphere was relaxing. I couldn't help but notice how this restaurant resembled the restaurant where we first met. This restaurant was on the pier as well, with a more romantic setting; it also seemed abnormally quiet for a weekday. We were seated at a long oval-shaped table surrounded by about twenty empty chairs. I looked around the restaurant and was impressed with the crystal chandeliers hanging from the ceiling and the waiters standing near every table, awaiting each diner's request. My heart beat uncontrollably but I tried not to show my nervous expression on my face.

"Hello, ma'am, you are looking stunningly beautiful tonight, by the way. May I start your night off with a beverage of your choice?" I looked up at the small-framed man wearing thick glasses. I thought about wine but was reminded of my experience a few nights ago.

"Thank you. I would like a virgin strawberry daiquiri." The waiter acknowledged my request with a nod, as his hands remained behind his back. He looked over at Ahmad.

"And for you, sir? By the way, you and your wife make a beautiful couple." Ahmad didn't bother to correct him, neither did I; it felt good to labeled as his wife.

"I'll have Hennessey on the rocks, and I appreciate the compliment. I found the greatest treasure that I plan on keeping." The waiter smiled and nodded his head to signify his exit from the table.

"Maad, why did they seat us at such a large table?" I whispered. By now, my palms were sweaty and I could hear my heart beating through my ears. I continued staring at Ahmad's lips, but they weren't moving. I overheard John Legend's song, "*All of Me*, playing softly throughout the restaurant speakers. It was such a nice coincidence, that song was playing right then.

Ahmad's lips remained stiff as he stood up and got down on one knee in front of me. Before I understood what was happening, I saw both our friends and family walking towards our table with flowers, balloons, and cameras. My hands were shaking uncontrollably as I tried to control the tears attempting to fall.

"April, you are my everything. I knew I wanted to spend the rest of my life with you since our first date. You deserve the best and I know I am fully capable of providing that, if you allow. Please share my world, and I promise that I will always hold your heart tenderly close to mine. Will you spend the rest of your life with me?"

Ahmad was on one knee in front of me, and I was blinded, not only by my tears but also by flashing camera lights. I managed to open my mouth.

"Yes! Yes, I will marry you, Maad! Our bond is unbreakable and unbelievable. I can't see my life without you."

My voice quivered and my hands were shaking as he slid the four-carat round solitaire ring on my finger. It was a perfect fit; I bet Kesha told him my ring size. I wiped my eyes and stood up to hug and kiss him. We embraced each other, followed by everyone else bombarding us with hugs and poses for camera shots.

"Congratulations, honey! Now you finally joined the club!" Kesha flashed her ring finger, and we both laughed and hugged.

"Girl, I'm mad you didn't tell me about this! I will definitely get you back!" I pointed at Kesha and gave her the evil eye as I spoke.

"My baby is all grown up now!" I could recognize that thick Jamaican accent from a mile away. I turned around and hugged my mom as tight as I could. I hadn't seen her in over a month, and I had no idea that she was here, or even aware of the engagement party. I can't believe Ahmad went through all this to have such important people show up.

"Ma! I am so glad you're here!" We embraced.

"You know I wouldn't miss this day for the world!" Our embrace was cut short by a deep voice with a French accent from a distance. My dad is from St. Lucia, so he speaks Creole French. I was never taught the language, but I eventually caught on through exposure.

"Look at my beautiful princess! I'm so happy for my baby!" My dad's six-foot seven-inch frame towered over my body. I loved hugging my dad. Although my mom and dad's relationship ended when I was a child, they maintained a positive relationship as my parents.

"Thanks, Daddy! I'm so glad that you are here." I tried to control the tears that formed in my eyes. Although I was closer to my mom, the bond between a father and daughter is one that is unexplainable and unbreakable.

"I can't imagine missing this moment." The smile on my dad's face as he spoke was priceless. We embraced before I made my way around the table, greeting everyone.

After everyone was settled and seated, we placed our orders. The night was full of laughter, conversation, and delicious food. Every now and then, I would glance at Ahmad and make eye contact. Each moment our eyes connected, my heart raced. I can honestly say this night was one of the best nights of my life. As I looked around at all the smiling faces, I knew that I would never forget this night; love filled the restaurant tonight.

After we all had eaten and watched everyone leave the restaurant, it was finally time for me to reveal my surprise to Ahmad. The ride back home from the restaurant felt way better than the ride to the restaurant. I was on a natural high and my heart and mind were finally of one accord. I massaged Ahmad's manhood during the ride home and warmed his muscles with my mouth.

When we walked into the house, I didn't give Ahmad a chance to settle down before I started ripping his clothes off. I needed to feel him inside of me. I used my tongue to undo each button on his shirt while my hands pulled down his already unzipped pants. As I pulled his top off, his pants slid down to his ankles and rested on top of his loafers. My hands roamed his thighs while I placed wet kisses on his groin. His moans confirmed what his body felt. I didn't hesitate to take him fully into my mouth. I tightened my lips around his rod and sucked and slobbered to mimic the wetness of my vagina. The faster I went, the more I felt his muscles tighten. I continued at a steady pace and only slowed down when I felt he wanted to release. Ahmad ran his fingers through my hair and moaned. I quickened my pace as he hit the back of my throat. His moans increased and so did the sound of my mouth. Ahmad exploded as I continued to suck and lick him dry. I didn't want to waste any of his sweetness. I stood up and smiled while Ahmad gathered himself.

"I'll be in the shower, babe. Wait for me in the bedroom after you freshen up." I made sure each word rolled off my tongue while I seductively stared at Ahmad. I winked at him before I turned around and walked upstairs.

Ahmad had three full bathrooms in his house, so I knew he would use one while I used the other. That night was the best love making I had experienced in a long time. The lingerie I wore in the bedroom lasted for all of five minutes before it was taken off. We made love all night, and into the early hours of the morning.

When I woke up, one side of my face was more sensitive than the other. I lifted my head and realized that I was lying on my ring finger. The ring appeared more beautiful this morning than it did last night. The rays of sunlight through the curtains made the diamond sparkle and sent a glare across my eyes. I held my hand up and smiled. I cannot remember ever being this happy and at peace. I got out of bed and walked downstairs, following the music I heard coming out of one of the bedrooms downstairs. Walking down the hallway, I observed just how articulate Ahmad is. Each painting was the same size and they were evenly spaced. I stopped in front of the bedroom, and watched Ahmad through the open doorway, where he had set up a workout room with a cardio machine, dumbbells, pull-up bar, and weight bench. I watched Ahmad do pull-ups; the amount of sweat running down his back confirmed my thoughts that he had been working out for a while this morning. He didn't notice me staring at him.

"Look at my sexy fiancé!" I licked my lips and stared as Ahmad brushed the locs out of his face and walked over and kissed me.

"Good morning, wifey! It's always good to see you first thing in the morning."

Ahmad slapped my butt and squeezed it.

"Likewise, babe. It is always good to be here every morning," I said.

"That's nice to know, Queen. I been thinking about us and I need you here with me. I know you mentioned moving your business here. All I'm saying is that I'm ready when you are," Ahmad said.

Those words were all I needed to hear. I'd been planning in my head to move to Alabama but wasn't sure if Ahmad was ready for me to move in with him. I didn't want Ahmad to feel pressured or obligated, but knowing he felt the same way confirmed my feelings.

"Hubby, I have been waiting for you to say those words for the longest. I will work towards moving here, and I don't want to be without you either."

We hugged each other in the tightest embrace. I didn't care that he was so sweaty; in that moment, I was blissful.

CLEAR SKIES

"ONE AREA IN LIFE WE MUST LEARN HOW TO BE, IS GRATEFUL."

The next weeks went fast. I opened another office in Birmingham, Alabama while the main office was in the Buckhead district in Atlanta, Georgia. My current clients remained faithful, and my clientele in Alabama increased though references. With all the ripping and running, I felt more exhausted than ever before. Some days I found myself sleeping at my work desk or waking up late for work. My favorite foods and wine nauseated me. I made an appointment with my doctor that was scheduled for this afternoon. I don't want to go, but I need to go. When I am not feeling well, it's always best to visit my doctor to ensure I am not having a flare up of my autoimmune disease.

The fear of my health condition worsening caused me to panic. I pulled into the parking lot of my doctor's office and let the car idle for a while. I thought about when I was diagnosed with systemic lupus a few years ago and how that diagnosis changed my life forever. The fear that my condition may have worsened caused my eyes to water. *April, get yourself together. No weapon formed against me shall prosper,* I repeated aloud to myself before walking into the doctor's office.

I signed in and waited to be called into the exam room. After I signed in, the nurse handed me a urine cup and a few blood sample tubes with my name and Social Security number on them. Since this was my first visit with a doctor since I moved away from Georgia, the doctor requested I take additional lab tests. I verified that the information listed was correct and took the urine cup into the bathroom. The physician's protocol is for all female patients to give a urine sample unless they are on some sort of birth control. After my first miscarriage, I dreaded the thought of a pregnancy test because I knew I would never carry another baby. I placed the full cup into the aluminum tray in the bathroom before walking into the lab next door to give blood samples. I observed the needle seep into my skin and pull out in one motion. The dark red fluid filled all five tubes, then I placed a cotton ball on the injection site and applied pressure. Afterwards, the nurse guided me back into the waiting room. My mind raced a mile a minute. The stack of magazines on the table did little to relax my mind. I pulled my cellular phone out of my purse and texted Kesha.

Me: Hey, girl, I'm at my doctor's appointment now. I'm kind of worried, but I hope I receive good news.

Kesha: It's normal to be concerned, but everything will be fine. I told you it is all the stress from moving. You must learn to give your body a break sometimes.

Me: I'm not stressed. Well, at least I don't feel like I am.

Kesha: In the past three months, have you slept as much as you should? Have you been eating like you usually do?

Me: No. Not really.

Kesha: Exactly! It's called stress. Once you have everything moved to

Alabama, you will be back to normal. When did you say you will have everything moved?

Me: Next week. I can't wait either! I'm going to need a mini vacation after next week. We should plan a couple's retreat!

Kesha: That sounds like a damn good plan! Between Robert and me trying to plan a wedding and have babies at the same time, I sometimes feel like I'm losing my mind! LOL!

Me: Girl, you and Rob are way overdue with planning a family. That should have already occurred. Honey, I just feel so blessed. Ahmad has helped me out tremendously with the transition. It could have been way more difficult. I could have been running around looking like wild woman snatching my hair out!

Kesha: LOL! That's funny! That's how you know you got a good man when you don't have to ask him to care about you. Trust me, April, you have been a blessing to me with helping plan this wedding. I know it's hard to deal with me when my mind continuously changes.

Me: You know you're my girl! I'm just happy that you all finally decided to take it to the next level.

Kesha: Aww, thanks, Chica! Now enough of the mushy stuff. What's going on over there? Have you seen the doctor yet?

Me: Not yet. I have been here for about two hours, gave a urine sample and blood sample. I guess they are testing everything now.

Kesha: Oh, okay. Keep me updated!

Me: I will.

"April?" The nurse called into the lobby.

I stood up and followed the nurse into the exam room. I sat on the exam table and waited for the doctor to enter the room.

"Hey, April! Nice to see you. How have you been?" The doctor reached his hand out for me to shake. He placed his thick brown rectangular glasses on his nose, and read over a few sheets of paper.

"I've been well, just extremely tired," I said.

"Well, that's understandable. I looked over your lab results. All your tests came back normal, except for one. Your urine test came back positive with an extremely high hCG level," The doctor smirked.

"Um, okay, so what does that mean?" I said. The term hCG sounded familiar, but I couldn't quite figure out where I had heard that term before. He needed to stop with all the medical talk and let me know what was up.

"April, you're pregnant, and according to your hCG levels and this chart right here, you are about three months along."

The doctor held up a pregnancy chart that showed a baby's development from the moment of conception up until birth.

"THREE MONTHS! Pregnant? Wow, this is so not the right time. Oh my gosh. Oh my gosh." I rocked back and forth, rubbing my hands together in shock. I would love to have Ahmad's baby, but I just didn't think it would happen this soon. How could I be pregnant?

"Have you been using protection or any form of birth control?" The doctor raised his eyebrows as he spoke, seemingly asking a common-sense question. I wanted to say obviously not, and shove that chart down his throat, but I decided against that idea. The doctor wrote down a few brands of prenatal vitamins and gave me the rundown of what I already knew about pregnancy before I left the office.

My walk to the car seemed farther than normal, and the sun felt hotter than normal. The doctor's words resonated in my mind, *three months pregnant*. As I pondered, reality hit me. Three months ago, I was with Chris and Ahmad. The thought of everything sent the food in my stomach hurling out of my mouth and onto the pavement. The heat outside made what was on the pavement resemble oatmeal. I wiped my mouth with the back of my hand as I tried to compose myself. This cannot be possible; my past sexual experiences with Chris never resulted in a pregnancy. Chris couldn't possibly be the father, or could he? I thought about that drunken night I had with Chris and realized that we had not used protection. I was on birth control at that at that time, so I doubt Chris is the father. The thought of it all nauseated me. Ahmad and I never used protection, so he could and should be the Father. I am disgusted with myself and my situation. I sat in the driver's seat, held the steering wheel, and cried. How could I possibly be so stupid! My phone vibrated, and it was Kesha calling me. As much as I wanted to keep this secret, I had to tell someone.

"Hello?" My voice was hoarse from crying.

"Oh my goodness! You sound horrible. What's wrong?" Kesha spoke with concern. It was time to tell the truth.

"Kesha, I'm three months pregnant." I couldn't control my tears as the truth fell out of my mouth.

"That's great news, April! I'm so happy for you. Rob and I have been trying. You shouldn't be sad," Kesha said.

"I don't know who the father is." I pulled a napkin out of my glove compartment to wipe my nose.

"Wait, hold on. Let me pull over. I don't think I heard you clearly. Either my mind is playing tricks on me or there is some serious shit you've been hiding from me!"

Kesha had every right to be upset. I couldn't even argue with her. If shit hit the fan, I knew she would have my back but I had to tell her the truth.

"What you heard is right. I don't know who the father is." I proceeded to tell her the entire story about my night with Chris. How he looks, how we met, our entire history up until three months ago. I didn't hold anything back. When I finished telling her, I felt like a burden had lifted off my shoulders after these years of keeping this secret. Kesha stayed silent for a while.

"Wooooooooow! April, I can't believe you kept that secret from me for so long. I would never judge you. I feel sad right now. Chris sounds like he would have been the perfect man for you if he had been available. I'm sorry that you went through all this alone. Just think positive and focus on Ahmad being the father. As of now, Ahmad is the father and will be. Has Chris tried to contact you? Are you going to tell him?" Kesha hit some valid points that had me thinking.

"Chris calls or texts me just about every day. He even sends emails. He keeps leaving messages that he has something important to tell me, but I don't respond or answer his calls. He knows that I am in the process of moving and I guess he learned of my new location since I moved my business to Alabama. Kesha, I just don't want to open those doors right now, and I'd rather leave well enough alone."

I started the ignition. I had calmed down and was focused enough to drive.

"I completely understand. It is all your decision. You are my girl no matter what! Now get your ass home and share the news with your future husband, honey!"

I laughed. Kesha always had a way of making me feel better.

"You're right, girl, I'm trippin. Thanks for the advice, and I love you, Kesha."

"Love you too. Drive safe and call me later." We hung up, and I drove home to see my hubby and tell him the good news.

KESHA

I needed time for everything to marinate. It amazes me that April held onto that secret for such a long time, without telling me. It hurt me to hear it, but I couldn't make it about me. That would be selfish of me. It was clear that April deeply loved Chris at some point in her life. If Ahmad wasn't in the picture and Chris was single, I have no doubt that they would be married. No woman in her right mind would deal with an unavailable man for that long, if she didn't deeply love him. Chris and April had history, deep history. She described him to the tee. I felt that I could recognize him even if I hadn't seen him before. I hope, for April's sake, that Ahmad is the father of her baby. Ahmad loves April with all his heart; his love is displayed through his actions. In the midst of April moving to Alabama, she never placed my wedding planning on hold or took a break from planning. Now that I know she is pregnant, I plan on a hiring a professional wedding planner. I know that idea won't go well with April, but she needs a break, and I do too.

Since Rob and I agreed to start a family, Rob's been having sex with me relentlessly. A few nights ago, we discussed the idea of taking our time with starting a family and not rushing the process. I learned that the moment that you stop trying is usually the time everything works out. We were sick and tired of being sick and tired, and finally decided to relax and let nature take its course. Now that everything is more natural and not so rushed, our lovemaking is back to normal, and it's unforgettable. Thinking about my man stirred up a wave of excitement inside of me, and I was ready to get home and lie in his arms. I made a mental note to call April tomorrow, I was sure she would be busy tonight with Ahmad. These next few months should be quite interesting.

APRIL

*A*fter I spoke with Kesha, a weight was lifted off my chest. So many thoughts went through my mind at once; I had to get myself together before I saw Ahmad. I pulled up to the house and flipped open the car's sun visor to look in the mirror. My eyes were puffy from crying, but weren't red anymore. I closed the visor and said a little prayer before walking into the house. The smell of food made my mouth moisten and my stomach turn from hunger. Ahmad was in the kitchen but he heard me come through the front door.

"Hey, babe!" Ahmad yelled from the kitchen.

"Hey, hubby, what are you doing in the kitchen?" I spoke calmly.

I didn't have the energy to yell, I was hoping that he heard me speaking at this tone. I took my shoes off and walked towards the kitchen.

"I'm not doing too much, just fixing a chicken salad. You look a little tired. Are you okay? How did the doctor's appointment go?"

Ahmad's look of concern caused knots to form in my stomach. I watched as he wiped his hands on the dish towel and walked towards me.

"Actually, there is a reason why I have been so tired lately. The doctor ran a few tests and one was abnormal…" My voice trailed off.

"What do you mean, abnormal?" Ahmad said.

"The urine test came back positive and… I'm pregnant." I looked down as I spoke for fear of his reaction. Before I could regain my composure, Ahmad swooped me off my feet and spun me around in the air. He had the brightest smile.

"We are having a baby! This is the best news I have heard my entire life! I am so glad you are my lady and my child's mother." His last few words stung, but I could not allow my thoughts to show on my face. *Lord, please let this baby be Ahmad's, I know it will break his heart if it isn't his baby,* I thought. I embraced Ahmad and kissed him. It wasn't long before our kiss turned into passionate love making on the kitchen table. This was our beginning, and my joy that I'd been waiting for all my life.

NEW LIFE

"THE ONLY THING CONSTANT IN THIS WORLD IS CHANGE."

*D*ays turned into weeks and weeks turned into months. I am now eight months pregnant. I woke up to the smell of a hot breakfast. I rolled onto my side and stared at the plate of food on the nightstand. These days, I am very uncomfortable lying on my side, so I always sleep on my back. The smell of the food caused my baby to move around in my belly. My belly is the size of a basketball. Most people wouldn't notice that I am pregnant if they are standing behind me, but once I'm viewed from the front or side, they can see that my belly is huge! I have maintained my nice shape because I continue working out. I can't run as often as I would like to, but I walk a few miles daily.

I rolled over onto my back and stared at the ceiling, meditating. Each morning that I awake, I take some time to myself to thank God that I am alive and blessed. I can't believe that time has gone by so fast, and I am grateful for everything in my life. Due to the success of my business in Georgia and Alabama, I had to hire another advisor in Georgia and expand my office in Alabama. Kesha's wedding is less than two months away, while Ahmad and I plan for our wedding to be held within a year.

I officially moved to Alabama and was at peace in my life. I finally felt complete. After my daily meditation, I ate my breakfast and looked around the house for Ahmad. The smell of paint instantly hit my nose after I opened the bedroom door; I followed the scent into the baby's room. I stood admiring Ahmad as he painted the baby's room a beautiful soft yellow color. We want the sex of our newborn to be a surprise, so we stuck with neutral colors for everything, down to the clothes. We decided to name our baby Asha if I have a girl or Ahmad if I have a boy. We want our children to keep their African names and not the names forced upon our ancestors through slavery.

I rubbed my belly and looked around the baby room, pleased with the progress we've made with decorations. I looked down at my toes and reminded myself to meet up with Kesha at the nail salon later today. Kesha's wedding planning is going great, the wedding will be held in St. Croix, Virgin Islands. Although Kesha did not want me to continue planning the wedding because of undue stress, I involved myself in the planning anyway but did not make it obvious enough for Kesha to notice.

The random calls to Ahmad's phone subsided but didn't cease. I asked Ahmad about the phone number, and he said sometimes the person on the other end wouldn't speak, so he planned on changing his number soon, and other times he refused to answer the relentless calls. Chris stopped calling me, but he continued sending weekly emails; some I read, and others I deleted. I wondered what he needed to tell me, but I quickly stopped entertaining the thought.

"Maad, I'm going to run to the grocery store and buy some

more fruit. You want anything in particular?" I leaned against the doorway as I spoke. This baby is weighing me down, literally.

"Nah, babe, I'm good. You love eating fruits, huh? At least I know both of my babies are healthy. Let me wash up and come with you. Give me a few," Ahmad said.

"You are right about that, healthy and strong! You don't have to come with me hubby, I shouldn't be gone long. I want you to finish painting the baby's room. Our baby will be here anytime now."

Ahmad walked up and hugged me from behind while swaying his hips from side to side. The control he had on my body made my hips move with his, as we danced to music that only we could hear.

"I love my wife, my family, my life. I am glad you are a part of me and I am a part of you."

Ahmad gently whispered this into my ear, and planted kisses on my neck. His soft lips sent tingles down my spine and caused my hair to rise on the back of my neck. My nipples hardened through my thin T-shirt, and the pressure between my legs grew. Ahmad ran his hands down the inside of my thighs and slapped my ass that jiggled under my tight T-shirt. My senses heightened, and my pussy lips pulsated for him to be inside of me. I placed one leg on the chair that Ahmad used for balance while he painted the ceiling, and tooted my behind up. Ahmad licked my thighs and pussy, pulled his gym shorts down, and gave me his full thickness. The sensation of him pounding me from behind and the smell of paint, sweat, and anticipation made me lose control. With each stroke, my fluids ran down his thickness and dropped onto the chair. Ahmad bent down, licked up my pussy juice running down my leg, and lay down with his back on the floor. I assumed the position. I saddled Ahmad and ground my hips into him as low as I could go, while slowly clenching my pussy muscles on his dick each time I rotated my hips. Our lips never parted as we kissed and my hips rotated even faster. Just the thought of him inside of me and how his hands squeezed and grabbed my ass, brought my second orgasm to another level. I used my hands to hold his wrist onto the floor while I sat up and bounced on his hard rod. The pain and pleasure forced me to lean my head back. The ends of my hair were soaked with sweat and my hair was no longer in a ponytail. Our skin slapping against each other was music to my ears. I looked down at my man's sculpted chest, his tensing confirmed that he was about to release his seed yet again inside of me. I rode even faster and dropped my hips onto his waist while my pussy muscles squeezed and pulled with each stroke. Ahmad moaned my name, as I felt all the warm goodness fill up my insides, and I knew it was a job well done. We lay on the floor in the baby's room, holding each other as though we were lying on our king size mattress. I was over-flooded with emotions and couldn't wait for my bundle of joy to get here.

"Hubby, the baby is jumping like crazy. I guess he or she is upset because I haven't picked up those fruits yet." I smiled.

"I noticed that too. My hands have been on your belly the entire time. You might want to get those fruits before both of you get upset with each other," Ahmad chuckled.

"That is so true! Let me shower and get myself together so I can rush back home to my man." I leaned over and kissed Ahmad as I struggled to get up and waddled to the bedroom.

After my shower, I put on a multi-colored maxi dress, threw my curly hair into a pony tail and walked out the door. The weather felt nice outside; the breeze, just right, and the birds chirping brought a sense of peace over me. I inhaled the air deeply before I walked to the car. Reflecting on my life, I would have never guessed any of this would have happened. I'd been through so much in my life that I gave up on love, and the happiness that surrounded it, until I met Ahmad. I believe that true love is finding someone who can and will love you through your imperfections; this person who is willing to make that sacrifice will become your soul mate. I adjusted my shades, stepped inside the car, and put on my seat belt. I was so busy humming gospel songs that I didn't feel the need to turn the radio on. As I sang those songs, a feeling came over me, and I knew I truly missed going to church and listening to the choir. It was something about gospel music that uplifted the soul. I decided to drive downtown to the fruit market. Just as I pulled behind a car in the turning lane onto Broadway Avenue from 18th street, my cellular phone rang. The Bluetooth automatically connected through my car speakers. I was aggravated because there was so much traffic on the road this afternoon.

"Hello!" I didn't care who was on the phone at that moment.

"April, can you talk?" That voice brought the same tingles through my body that it did years ago.

"Yes? Who is this?" I pretended that I didn't recognize the voice on the other end.

"It's Chris. I really need to talk to you. Where are you? Can I meet you? I'm in Alabama at a conference downtown." Chris tried to push his statement through one breath.

"What do you want, Chris?" I waited behind the car in the turning lane that wasn't moving.

"I want to see you. I need to see you. Please, April, just five minutes of your time? I know you're living in Alabama and have moved on with your life, but I just need to speak with you face-to-face," Chris pleaded.

"Chris, I am eight months pregnant and engaged to be

married. There is nothing to talk about. You and I are done. I have moved on with my life." I honked my horn at the car in front of me that still hadn't turned.

"Wow! Congratulations! I still would love to see you. I am on Eighteenth Street and Madison Avenue. Are you near the downtown area?"

Between Chris's questions and this car in front of me, my patience was at an all-time low.

"It doesn't matter. Say what you need to say!"

I honked at the car again and noticed they put on their hazard lights. I looked out of the driver's side mirror and my rearview mirror, to make sure I was clear to go around the stalled car.

"April, I am so very sorry that I waited so long, and I know you have moved on, but I haven't. My divorce was finalized six months ago. I've been living alone and not dating anyone. I am and have always been in love with you. I don't care that you are pregnant, I will love you and that new life inside of you as my own. Please just speak with me in person for five minutes?"

The words Chris spoke brought tears to my eyes. What I had been hoping to hear for two years, I finally heard at the worst time. I didn't understand why the tears began falling or why my heart felt torn. I finally saw a clear opening to go around the car in front of me and made a right turn onto Broadway Avenue.

"I am on Eighteenth Street and Broadway Avenue. We can meet up at the fruit market on Broadway Avenue," I said. I was now very curious about this urgent news he needs to tell me.

I didn't see any oncoming traffic nor the semi-trailer truck merge into the lane as I made the right turn. Everything happened so fast. I heard tires screeching, I felt glass break my skin, and my chest tightened from struggling to breathe. The last voice I heard was Chris calling my name before I saw pure darkness.

≈

I awakened to muffled words, but couldn't open my eyes. While she spoke, I tried to digest everything Kesha was telling me. When she mentioned the doctor saying I needed to fight, I realized that I was in a hospital bed. Fear came over me while I thought about my family, and wondered if they were truly doing as well as Kesha said they were. I heard someone come into the room, then checking my vitals and changing my tubes. How long have I been in the hospital? Why is Kesha crying? I didn't feel like I was in bad condition. I just felt extremely sore. The nurse said something to Kesha about me needing rest; I felt something cold go through my veins as I dozed off.

≈

I watched the butterfly land on my shoulder with its pretty yellow-and -black wings, and then fly off. From a distance, I heard a familiar voice that made me smile.

"April, you've grown into such a beautiful woman." I turned around to see my great -grandmother, Dada, staring at me and smiling. Her beautiful long gray hair plaited down to her waist. Her soft brown skin and high cheekbones looked the same as I remembered when I was a young girl. I ran towards her and gave her the longest hug and kiss on the cheek.

"Dada, I have missed you so much. It is so beautiful and peaceful here." I looked into Dada's beautiful brown eyes that were an exact reflection of mine.

"Yes, it is beautiful here, but you cannot stay. I will see you again, but you cannot stay now." She held my hand and pointed towards the

sky. The sun was breathtaking; it was very bright but sent such a strong feeling of love into the atmosphere. The yellow dandelions moved with each turn of the wind. We closed our eyes as we inhaled the fresh air and let the breeze flow through our hair…

～

"She must go into surgery now or we will lose the baby!" I woke up to hearing all kinds of noises around me. The voices sounded more like panic than anything else. I felt the hospital bed moving. I still couldn't see anyone but I heard everything.

"The baby is in distress, and the heart rate has dropped. We have to do an emergency Cesarean section," the male voice said.

"But, Doctor, none of her family members are here to consent." The female voice sounded concerned, I assumed she was a nurse.

"It doesn't matter. Right now, it is life or death. Do as I say and prep this patient for surgery! Ensure the OB and neonatal intensive care unit is notified just in case we have any emergency with the baby!" the male said before closing a door behind him.

After that conversation, I didn't hear much of anything besides beeping sounds, and I smelled the scent of Iodine. Did they just say my baby is in distress? I tried to jump up and yell, but I couldn't move. *Please, God, don't let my baby die. Please, please I beg you,* I pleaded with God in my mind. I heard a lot of beeps and muffled voices coming from people around me, and then something was placed on my face as I drifted off once again.

AHMAD

$\mathcal{I}$ was at the hospital every night for the past two weeks. I never left April's bedside, not even for a moment. Last night, Kesha and Rob had to practically push me out of April's hospital room to go home and rest. I promised that I would sleep at home just for that night, but would be at the hospital first thing in the morning. Kesha told me she would leave the hospital early the next morning to grab more clothes from her home and would be back by noon. I tossed and turned all night. The house felt dead and lonely without April. I couldn't manage sleeping in our bedroom, so I slept in the baby's room, and cried. I blamed myself for everything; I shouldn't have let her go to the grocery store alone. If I had stopped painting the baby's room and gone to the grocery store for her, maybe the accident would not have happened. Guilt and pain overwhelmed me as I leaned with my back against the wall in the baby's room and slowly slid to the floor in tears. It seemed like the walls in the house felt my wails and absorbed every bit of hurt that came out of my mouth. My wails echoed throughout the house and haunted my mind as I clutched my face with my hands and cried.

I hadn't realized that I had dozed off in the baby's room until my cell phone rang.

"Hello?" My voice was weak from crying, but I managed to answer the phone as clearly as possible.

"Hey, Ahmad. I am at the airport. You said you would be here, but I assume you probably overslept." I looked at the watch on my wrist and jumped up, still a little dizzy from lack of sleep. The brightness from the sun greeted me through the window screen.

"Oh, Ma. I am so sorry. These past few weeks have been very long, and I dozed off. Please forgive me. I am on my way to the airport now. I should be there in no more than fifteen minutes." I completely forgot that April's mom's flight landed this morning. April's mom had been here last week, but had to leave for a few days to sort out her farm business in Jamaica. The entire immediate family planned on visiting April today and praying together.

I gathered the little strength that I had left, grabbed my car keys, and walked out of the house.

"It's okay. I know you're tired, son. I will see you soon," Ma chuckled.

She was always understanding, even when under so much pressure. We hung up, and I raced to the airport to pick her up. Traffic wasn't bad on the highway today. I arrived sooner than I expected at the airport. I saw Ma sitting on the bench, rocking back and forth; I assumed she probably was humming some spiritual hymn as she usually did to calm her mind. I pulled up to the curb, parked, and got out to get her luggage.

"Hey, Ma! It's nice to see you. How was the flight?" We embraced each other. The closest feeling, I have to April is her mother, and I felt much more at peace with her being around me now. I opened the passenger door for her to sit, and then closed the door. I grabbed her luggage and placed it in the trunk before we pulled off towards the hospital.

"The flight wasn't bad at all. I just want to see my baby girl. All three of my babies: you, her, and the baby." We chuckled; a sense of humor was a great blessing right then.

"April is holding on. Well, I pray they both will come through this. Kesha stayed with April last night and was going to head home this morning, to grab a few more clothes once I relieved her." I looked at my watch on my wrist; it was going on 8:00 a.m. with no phone call from anyone at the hospital. I started to feel uneasy.

"You act like you're pulling guard duty! *Relieve her!* That's a funny statement. Trust me, April isn't going anywhere!" Ma shook her head and smiled, she is always so optimistic. I just hope this time she is right. In the middle of our conversation, my cell phone rang. I answered and it was Kesha, frantically yelling on the other end.

"Ahmad, you need to get here now! They took April into surgery. Rob and I went downstairs to get breakfast, and literally within ten minutes, we came back to her room and she was gone. They told us the baby was in distress and they need to do an emergency Cesarean section. Please hurry! I feel like I'm about to lose my mind," Kesha sobbed into the phone. I wanted to cry, but I had to maintain my composure.

"Kesha, calm down. We are less than ten minutes away. I will be there shortly, okay?" I tried my best to stay calm on the outside, but I was scared shitless on the inside.

"What's going on?" Ma had a concerned look on her face.

I briefed her on what Kesha just told me as I drove as fast as I could to the hospital. Ma didn't say a word, she just kept praying under her breath. When I parked in the hospital parking lot and ran upstairs, all I could think about was my family. I couldn't lose my wife and baby at the same time. Just the thought made me feel like I wouldn't be able to live. I didn't care that we weren't married yet. In my mind, April was my wife and always would be. We checked in at the front desk of the hospital and walked into April's room. To my surprise, the entire family was there with flowers, balloons, and cards. April's siblings, as well my siblings, were in the room. When I walked in, everyone looked up at me with sadness in their eyes.

I know that I looked a mess and I didn't care. I hadn't shaved in two weeks; I hadn't hit the gym or been eating healthy. My life was not my concern right then. My family leaving the hospital was my concern and my life. Everyone stood up and hugged me, one by one. Throughout this ordeal, Rob never left my side. Most nights he would sit in the corner of the hospital room and watch me hold April's hand and talk to her. Rob would be so silent that many nights, I forgot he was still in the room. I would talk to April about our vacation plans and tell her how I bought her a swimsuit and bought a few more outfits for the baby. I could swear that she heard me because, every now and then, her finger would move or her eye would twitch if I ask her to respond. I constantly reminded her that she had more life to live and we needed her here with us; hopefully, my words held some truth to it. My thoughts were interrupted when the doctor walked into the room.

"Mr. Okibo? Can I speak with you in a separate room?" The doctor looked around the room, waiting for someone to answer.

"Yes, that's me. How is she?" I stood up and walked towards the doctor, who led me into an adjacent room.

"Sir, she delivered a healthy eight-pound fifteen-ounce baby girl! Congratulations!" The doctor rubbed his hand on my shoulder, but didn't seem like he was finished talking. A worried expression crossed his face as his eyebrows creased.

"There is more...April did not hold up well after the surgery. She is in critical condition, and we transferred her to the ICU unit. Only three people are allowed in the room at a time, but I will make an exception seeing how loving your family is. April is a true fighter, but we must give her time to rest. As long as everyone else is out of her room by 8:00 p.m." The doctor paused after his statement.

I had so many questions. What does he mean by she is not holding up? I thought.

"What do you mean by April didn't hold up well? Where is the baby? Who can stay in her room after 8:00 p.m.?" I had so many questions that I didn't know where to start or end.

"April lost a lot of blood during the surgery, and her body is already weak. Her immune system is in overdrive, and her vitals aren't stable. The baby is in the nursery. I let the nurse know to be expecting you and two others that you choose. After 8:00 p.m., only one person is allowed in April's room, so you must let the front desk know prior to that time. I apologize that I have to deliver such sad news at one time." The doctor held his head down after he finished talking.

"Thank you, Doc, and I appreciate all your help and concern for my family. I will go see my daughter now and deliver this news to everyone else." The doctor nodded his head; I stood up and exhaled before exiting the room. It was time to relay the good and the grave news to everyone who was waiting.

After my verbal delivery, the room fell silent enough to hear a pin drop. If there was a ditch built in that room, a pond would form from all the tears. While everyone digested the information, I took that time to visit my daughter. April's mom and I took the elevator to the nursery unit. After going through what seemed like a special security clearance, we finally received our wristbands and I was able to hold my daughter. She is breath taking; her pretty brown eyes and head full of curly hair was a reflection of her mother. She stretched out her arms and little legs, while yawning and moving her head around until she looked up and stared at me. My vision blurred as my eyes filled with tears. I imagined April and I holding our daughter and talking, but then, I was the only one experiencing this feeling.

April had lost her first child and was not able to experience her second. By this time, I couldn't control myself, so April's mom grabbed my daughter out of my hands as I walked out of the nursery and broke down. *This couldn't be happening to me! Not right now! Not right now!* I felt so weak. All my muscles meant nothing in my body if my heart wasn't strong. I left Ma in the nursery and returned the wristband to the nurse. I walked towards the elevator to visit April in the Intensive Care Unit. The rest of the family was in the ICU waiting room, while Rob and Kesha waited downstairs so they could take turns visiting Asha.

KESHA

*R*ob and I waited downstairs while everyone else went to visit April in ICU. I had to see my niece first. I was sitting on the couch, lying in Rob's arms, when I noticed a gentleman standing in front of the door entrance, staring into the room. I guess he was wondering why there was an empty hospital bed and two people cuddling on the couch. I saw sadness in his eyes, and I also saw something else. This man looked familiar, way too familiar. I moved out of Rob's arms and stood up to walk towards the man who looked lost. As I got closer to his face, I stepped back in surprise.

"Chris?" I was hoping that I was seeing things and that the description I had been told didn't match the man standing in front of me.

"Yeah...Yes. That is my name. Is this April's room? I'm sorry if I am in the wrong room, but I have been trying to find my friend for the past two weeks, and the nurse pointed me in this direction." Chris stuttered and looked very nervous and confused. He looked as though he hadn't slept in days, maybe weeks.

"Yes, you have the right room. Let's step out and chat for a second."

I turned around and Rob gave me a look like he needed an explanation. I walked over to Rob and promised him that I would tell him all about this later and that this guy was a good friend of April's. After Chris and I walked around the corner, I explained to him that I was April's best friend, and when she found out that she was pregnant, she had explained the full background of their relationship to me. I also gave him an update of April's status in the hospital and that she had delivered her baby. I have never seen a grown man break down the way I saw Chris break down. The pain he displayed was way deeper than what I knew. His hurt brought tears to my eyes; I could only imagine how he was feeling on the inside. After he gathered himself, he asked me if he could see the baby. I knew he could only visit the nursery if I was with him.

We walked towards the elevator. During the elevator ride, Chris told me what he had been holding in for months, and about the last conversation he had with April. The secret he revealed to me about his divorce, brought tears to my eyes and I began to cry. I could see that he and April truly, deeply loved each other, but he waited too long to tell her what she always wanted and needed to hear. This situation was so sad and heartbreaking to me.

We went through a security section and then walked into the nursery, observing all the newborns until we saw Asha. She was the most active baby in the nursery. Her eyes stood out the most to me. When Chris leaned towards Asha and picked her up, I was in complete shock. They both had the same almond colored eyes with a hazel tint. The baby cooed in his arms, cuddled into his chest, and fell asleep as he rocked her. I was in awe and didn't know what to say. Chris looked over at me, then down at Asha, and spoke softly while she slept.

"Kesha, how am I going to tell April's fiancé that this is my daughter?" A tear rolled down his face and onto Asha's bib. I couldn't even respond to his comment as he handed me Asha and I took my turn holding her in my arms.

CHRIS

*E*verything happened so fast, the car accident, the birth, and now ICU. All my stress went out the window when I saw my daughter. There was an undeniable bond that I felt. Not only did she look like her mother, but those eyes were a direct reflection of mine. I had so many mixed emotions. Now that I had seen our daughter, the only missing piece was April.

Kesha told me the condition April was in and that her hair was shaven because of the brain surgery, due to swelling from the car accident. I didn't care how she appeared at that moment; April was always the beautiful angel that captured my heart years ago. I was April's soul mate. She told me years ago why she stopped believing in soul mates, but I knew I was her soul mate. I just could not explain that to her because of the situation I was in at that time.

I thought Asha was a beautiful, exotic name, and it fit our daughter perfectly. While Kesha held Asha, I grabbed my phone and Googled the name to find out the meaning. Asha is an Eastern

African name that means "life" in Swahili. I placed my phone back in my pocket in deep thought; it amazed me how April chose such a perfect name for a perfect child, that she was not able to see or hold. I shook my head, hoping it would clear all the thoughts going through my mind. *How would I ask April's fiancé for a DNA test? Does he know about me? Who will take care of my daughter?* I didn't know which question I wanted to entertain first.

"Hey, Chris, Asha is knocked out and I need to hurry home to grab more clothes. I was supposed to go this morning, but April had the emergency surgery. I should be back within the next few hours. Is there anything else you need my help with?" Kesha's eyes showed sincere concern, and for the first time, I realized why April and Kesha were best friends. I could tell Kesha was the ride -or- die type for anyone she loved.

"I just would like to see April. I will deal with everything else later," I said.

"April is upstairs in ICU. Anyone can visit her until eight o' clock tonight, so you have enough time to visit if you'd like. I suggest you get yourself together before you make your way upstairs, though. Everyone should be leaving pretty soon to pick up dinner and meet at Ahmad's house later tonight." Kesha looked down at her watch and I knew she wanted to get on the road to beat rush hour traffic so she could be back in time.

"Thank you, Kesha. I deeply appreciate everything, and please take my number, and I will keep in contact with you." We exchanged numbers and saved it in our cell phones before we went our separate ways down the hall.

*I*f this doesn't sound like some crazy love triangle, then I don't know what one is. Everything Chris told me was true; I knew it was true based on how he described everything and the timeframe. Now it all made sense to me why April would act like she was in a relationship when I would try to hook her up on blind dates. April had been in love with this man, under the wrong circumstances. I felt so bad that my girl went through all this and was still going through more in this hospital. I was overcome with grief as I walked to the empty hospital room downstairs and met with Rob. As Rob and I walked to our car outside, I enlightened him on everything that I learned about Chris and April's relationship, all the way up until the pregnancy and current birth. Shock could not describe Rob's facial expression when I was finished. Rob didn't say anything the entire drive until we walked into our house.

"Damn, Kesha, everything just hit me. This is so jacked up. It's like all three of them are victims, and there is no one to blame because, at the end of the day they have this beautiful innocent little girl who needs love and attention."

I stared at Rob and agreed with his words. I never thought about it like that, but he was right.

"Wow, Rob, I never looked at it that way. But, I don't care who decides to love her, as long as my niece gets the love and attention that she needs, and if they can't figure it out, then Asha will definitely come with us!" It seemed like all this drama was something out of a television show, but all I cared about at that point was Asha and April. I didn't give a damn about how anyone was feeling about anything else. I also wanted to mention another point to Rob before he spoke again.

"Also, Robert, you cannot say anything to Ahmad about this. I know y 'all are like brothers but when it comes to love and babies, you have to stay out of it and let those two men figure it out for themselves. Promise me that you will not interfere?" I had my hand on my hips, waiting for an answer. I know how close Rob and Ahmad are, but I really needed him to let all of this play out on its own.

"Yes, babe, I promise. I can't deny that it will be hard for me to keep this secret but I will not get in the way this time. I will wait until Ahmad comes to me…if he comes to me." Rob exhaled and looked down.

I know he felt bad about everything, especially keeping such a deep secret away from his friend, but sometimes you have to keep secrets hidden to protect those you love.

"Thanks, Rob. Trust me, I know it will be hard for you. It's hard for me too, but we have to wait and let everything play out." I rubbed my hand across his face, lifted his head, and kissed his lips.

The drive home had been tough, but I was glad we had made

it home safely. Rob and I hadn't been intimate much these last few weeks, and my body was screaming for his attention. I was sure we could fit a little time in, for us. I grabbed his hand and led him to the bathroom. I could tell his body yearned for me just as much as I needed him. As we walked to the bathroom, we stripped off our clothes and made our way into the shower. His large hands roamed and massaged every inch of my body. Each area of my body he touched sent a different sensation through me. He used his fingers to explore my wetness as I lifted my ass to give him better access. His touch heightened my senses while I relaxed and enjoyed the attention. Rob didn't waste any time as he lifted me and pressed my body against the shower wall. I spread my legs as wide as I could to prepare for the pounding and pleasure I knew I was about to receive. I grabbed onto the shower rack above me as I felt his dick spread my pussy lips apart. The smoothness and thickness was unreal as my pussy spoke to him and released more slippery cream, preparing for the next stroke. The deeper he went, the wetter I became. The sound of the hot shower water, combined with the noise of our skin slapping together, made me hornier and yearn for more. My fingers dug into his back as he applied more pressure and bent his knees to grind slower and deeper inside of me. I couldn't take any more as my pussy muscles tightened and his strokes were steady.

"Oh yes, right there, daddy… Oh yes. Please don't stop, please don't stop." Every inch of my body felt hot. Just when Rob felt me about to climax, he picked up the pace and pounded me even harder. My ass jiggled against his groin while his balls slapped my pussy lips. I felt my wetness expand each time he pulled me higher up his dick before he pounded it back inside of me. I squeezed Rob as I came for what seemed like forever.

"Oooooh shit, babe. I feel your cream and know you like

daddy dick, don't you?" Rob pounded even harder, waiting for my response. His fingers dug into my ass cheeks as he continued to hold me up. I tried to respond but my mouth was so dry from me holding it open and breathing hard. I felt another orgasm coming.

"Daddy, I'm coming again!! Ugggggghhhhhhhhhhh," I moaned.

"Me too, babe!" Rob whispered before he released his seeds inside of me that my pussy drank all up. There was no liquid that dripped when he slowly placed my legs down. The love we had just made was long overdue. We finished our shower together, then Rob left the bathroom first to pack the clothes and get ready to head back to the hospital.

Once Rob stepped out of the bathroom, I closed the door and searched for the pregnancy test box I kept in the back of the bathroom cabinet. Lately, I've been very moody, but I didn't mention it to Rob because I didn't want him to get all excited for potential false pregnancy results. I opened the box, read the directions, sat on the toilet, and peed on the stick. During the next two minutes, I rested my head in my hands and waited. I thought about April and wondered how she was doing or what was going on in her mind at this time. After two minutes, I flipped the pregnancy stick over and saw a plus sign. I pulled the directions out of the trash, and read that a plus sign was positive for pregnant. My eyes widened. I covered my mouth and held my stomach, trying to hold in my scream of excitement. I thought about the last time I'd had my period, about two months ago. I didn't fear after two months because my periods were irregular, but this time, I felt differently and I now understood why. I left the pregnancy test on the counter and ran out of the bathroom with my robe on.

"Rob! Rob!" I yelled throughout the house like a mad woman.

Rob came running out of the kitchen and almost dropped the sandwich in his hand.

"Babe, are you okay? What's going on? Something wrong?" Rob stared, patting every inch of my body as if he were looking for wounds.

"Babe, I'M PREGNANT!" I jumped into his arms with excitement as he spun me around in a circle. I was beyond happy and couldn't wait to tell April. I know she can't talk right now but I knew she heard everything I said to her. I could just sense it. Rob was all smiles when he pulled away from me.

"We are having a fammmily. We're having a fammmily." He danced around in a circle with the sandwich still in his hand. I couldn't help but laugh.

"Really, Rob, you couldn't let that sandwich go, huh?" We laughed as I walked into the kitchen to grab the sandwich he made for me.

"Babe, are the clothes packed?" I asked with my mouth full of food.

"Yes, they are, and I am ready. Just waiting on you, slow poke. I mean slow mama!" Rob was already using my pregnancy to his advantage.

APRIL

"I'm so proud of you. You delivered a healthy baby girl, our healthy baby girl. She is beautiful, April, and looks just like you. She has these amazing brown eyes that are almond-colored, and she has thick curly hair. I know I'm going to have to fight these boys off her and you're gonna give her that mother-daughter talk," Ahmad spoke as he held my hand.

I heard everything he said but my body felt weak and tired. The only peace I had was knowing I had delivered my baby, a healthy strong baby girl. I pictured how she looked from the description Ahmad gave, and Chris came to mind. I didn't fight the thought that Chris could be the father anymore. I knew either man would be a great father to Asha, either way it went. I was tired of fighting at this point and needed peace. All my life, it seemed I was placed in bad situations that I did not ask for, but I was forced to deal with. I wanted so badly to speak to Ahmad, and I wanted him to hold me in his arms, but I could not move. I felt worse than before with a major headache. Ahmad continued talking but I couldn't hear him anymore as I felt my mind drift off again…

Lord, if you're listening, please take care of my family if it is time for me to go. I also ask that you forgive me for any wrong that I have done and do not hold my sins against my offspring. Amen.

~

"*I* see you're back again!" Dada displayed a bright smile on her face.

"Yes, Dada, I am back. I am so tired of fighting. I just want to rest now," I said. Dada's face showed sadness.

"I know you are tired, my baby. You will soon rest. Asha is beautiful and will be a true blessing to everyone around her. You shouldn't worry yourself over her. You will be there her entire life, just as I was with you." Dada ran her fingers through my hair. Her touch relaxed my mind and body. We were still in the same field of dandelion flowers. I saw a little boy running in the distance toward us; he couldn't be more than three years old. As he got closer, I noticed his curly hair and dark smooth complexion with the same brown eyes as Dada's. He stopped directly in front of me, held out his hand, and smiled.

"Mama, I have missed you and been waiting on you." I couldn't control the tears that flowed as I reached out and hugged him. He still smelled like his baby blanket. He hugged me back as we cried. I looked over at Dada, with tears in her eyes and a smile on her face.

"See, I told you. We were always here with you every step of the way." Dada held out her hand to both of us as she spoke. I reached my hand out to connect with Dada's and we all walked off into the dandelion flower field. I had never felt such joy and peace in my life. Now I can finally rest.

AHMAD

The more I spoke to April, the tighter she held on to my hand. Her eyelids fluttered more, as she had tried to open them but it never happened.

"I love you, April, Asha will always be taken care of. Please don't worry," I whispered in April's ear. I watched a tear fall from her eye, and saw her heart rate slow down on the monitor. All the medical staff ran in and tried to force me to leave the room. I didn't know what was going on and fought to stay in. I didn't care who was watching. I yelled and screamed April's name, with a mixture of tears and mucous on my face. I used all the strength I had to run back to her bedside, but security was called in and the guards pinned me onto the floor. The cold hospital floor against my face didn't stop me from yelling April's name. The weight of the four security guards and the position of my body forced my head to turn in the opposite direction, away from April's bed. I couldn't see what was going on, but I heard the commotion. Our family members were crying and some were screaming. I heard April's mom praying, and the doctors' voices.

"ONE...TWO...THREE"

"No pulse"

"We are losing her!"

"ONE...TWO...THREE"

"No pulse, Sir"

Those words resonated repeatedly until I heard a flat steady beep.

"She is gone at 6:52 p.m." Those were the last words I heard before footsteps walked past my head and I passed out.

KESHA

I was just about to take another bite of my sandwich when the phone rang. I picked up the cordless phone after the second ring.

"Hello?" I put the sandwich back on the plate and wiped my fingers with a napkin that Rob handed to me.

"Hey, Kesha, it's Ma. You may want to sit down for a second."

My stomach automatically felt queasy. I don't know if it was from the words or the food I had just eaten. I sat in the chair next to me and didn't know what to expect. Sometimes Ma could be so calm with sad news or good news.

"Kesha, April passed away at 6:52 p.m. The doctors did all they could. Her body was too weak after the b…." Everything became a blur to me after I heard that my best friend, my sister, my ace, was dead.

ROB

I sat on the couch when I heard Kesha talking on the phone, and then I walked over to Kesha to find out what was going on. After she sat in the kitchen chair, Kesha held the phone to her ear and did not move. What I witnessed next, I was not prepared for, but glad I had quick reaction skills. The cordless phone dropped out of Kesha's hand and hit the floor just as her body went limp, and she almost fell out of the chair before I caught her. I didn't know what to do and started to panic. I felt Kesha's pulse; her heart was still beating, she was breathing normally, and her face was wet with tears. I laid her on the couch and grabbed the phone. I needed to know who was on the other end and what they could have said to make her so upset.

"Hello? Hello? Kesha, are you there?" I knew it was Ma from her Jamaican accent.

"Hey, Ma, it's Rob. Kesha kind of passed out. She is breathing normally, but I'm about to wet a washcloth and wipe her face to wake her up. Is everything okay? Why is she so upset?" I leaned against the kitchen counter and turned on the sink, ran cool water, and wet a washcloth, awaiting on Ma's response.

"Robert, April passed away today at 6:52 p.m. The doctors tried all they could to revive her, but the stress from giving birth and everything else didn't allow her body to bounce back."

I couldn't believe what I had heard. I stood in shock and did not move. The water was still on and the washcloth was sitting inside of the sink, now soaked with water. Ma's voice was shaky, and she wept on the phone. All I could do was hold the phone to my ear and look over at Kesha, who had just woken up on the couch and was hysterically crying. Two women crying… one on the phone and one on the couch. I needed to call Ahmad. I knew he needed me the most right now.

CHRIS

I finally made my way to the Intensive Care Unit, and *nervous* was the best word to describe my feelings at the moment. The smell of death mixed with new life lingered in the air. *I hate visiting hospitals.* I received a wristband from the front desk and slowly walked down the hall to April's room. I peeked in and stared at the roomful of people whom I assumed were from both families. What caught my attention the most was when I saw April lying in bed and a man sitting next to her, stroking her hand and talking to her. His back was towards me, so he could not see me nor could he sense me staring at him. April's head was clean-shaven; her eyes were closed, and she had lost a lot of weight from being in the hospital bed for so long. Her stomach showed a pudge, and her arms looked slender.

I was overcome with grief as tears rolled down my face. I wanted to, at least, hug April. I needed to hug her and let her know I was there and that I had never left. I exhaled, wiped my face, and decided it was time to confront the truth. I was just about to step into the room when a nurse grabbed my hand and asked me to step outside because they needed to enter the room. What looked like ten doctors and nurses ran into the room at once and forced all the family members out of the room. All the family members were moved down the hall, but no one noticed me standing in the corner, still within view of the entire scene. I watched the man who was sitting next to April's bedside fight the security guards until they pinned him down on the ground and turned his head away from the scene. But I witnessed everything. I saw the doctors squeeze lubrication onto the two metal plates and place them on April's bare chest. I saw April's body jump up from the shock and then lie flat. The electric sensation caused her arms to flare up and fingers to move, but after each sensation, her body remained still. This continued for what seemed like five minutes before a white sheet was placed over her body. I didn't even notice the cries or screams around me because I, too, was in shock of what I had just witnessed. When I turned around and walked away from the room, my eyes made contact with an older beautiful woman who looked like April. I stopped, startled, thinking I was seeing things, until I looked at her lips and noticed she was mumbling prayers. She walked towards me and placed her hand on my shoulder.

"I know who you are. You do not have to fight for her love any more. She is already yours. Do not be afraid to reveal it." She squeezed my shoulder and then walked into the room and knelt next to the man on the floor, who was now screaming and crying. I was confused by her words and could barely walk down the hall because my tears blurred my vision. If it wasn't for Asha, I would have wanted to die right there next to April, the love of my life. But I had bigger things to worry about, and that was how I would get Asha back to me.

TWO MONTHS LATER...

awoke to the sounds of Asha crying in her room. Her afternoon naps seemed to get shorter and shorter. I picked Asha up and rocked her back and forth. Her dimples are so beautiful and she loves to smile whenever I look into her eyes. Holding my daughter always brought me a serene peace, and I felt April's spirit next to me. I tried to feed Asha, but she kept moving her head away from the bottle. Instead, she held on to my pinky finger and giggled. I looked at Asha and shook my head; my sleep didn't matter to me as long as my daughter was happy. My cell phone vibrating in the holster on my hip interrupted our bonding time. I pulled the phone off the holster and looked at the caller ID screen. I'd been avoiding this phone call for over a year. I guess it was time that I answered.

"Hello?"

"Ahmad? This is Nadine. I have been trying to reach you for over a year. There is something important we need to talk about."

Nadine's tone was serious and seemed urgent, but I didn't care for her urgency at the moment.

"Well, hello to you too, Nadine. I'm not in the mood at the moment to speak about anything. Just because a topic is urgent for you, does not mean that it is a priority for me." I was just about to hang up the phone until she spoke words that halted me in my tracks.

"Ahmad, you have two daughters, not one!" Nadine continued to speak, but I could not hear anything else that was said. I looked down at Asha in my arms, who was no longer smiling. A confused expression crossed my face. I had so many questions, and Nadine had better pray to God that she had all the answers...

SNEAK PEAK: THE SWEETEST SIN

PART II

Years have passed and Asha is now an adult figuring out how to put the pieces of her life back together.

There are many secrets exposed and hidden that Asha is determined to figure out. But the biggest secret of all, may tear her family apart. Find out in this final series how Asha, Ahmad, and Chris juggle death, life, and devastation, where time will reveal if blood is really thicker than water…

Coming Summer 2019!

EXCERPT

I am described as quiet or timid by most people who don't know me very well, but I am far from both. While others who recognize and understand my personality; never disrespect me. My name is familiar and respected in this neighborhood from the elders, down to the little children who haven't learned to form words yet. I had to make a name for myself, whether you find it good or bad. Growing up, I didn't have an older brother or sister to protect me nor did I mention any problems that I had with others to my dad. I learned to handle the majority of all my problems alone. If I ever needed help, I could always count on my best friend Kimberly. My name is Asha, but everyone calls me A or Ace. Mom's passed while giving birth to me and Pop's has been in my life ever since. I don't care about what anyone else says, no one can take the place of a mother's love. It doesn't matter, how long the woman was taking care of you. If you did not come out of her wound, then that special bond will not be there. I guess I can only speak for myself regarding that topic.

Although my dad plays an active role in my life daily, my grandmother is the closet feeling to having a mother. Don't get me wrong, I love my grandmother to death; Lord knows I will go through hell and high water just to maintain that beautiful smile on her face. But not a day goes by, that I don't think about my Mother. I was robbed of the chance to speak to my mother, yet miss her so much. My entire life I've felt my mother's presence. Many nights I have sat in my bedroom in dark silence, while only hearing the tiny squeaks of the house shifting or the breeze whistling its way under my bedroom window. And then I would hear her voice, clear as day.

When I was younger, I was so afraid when I heard my mother's voice because I didn't think it was normal. I thought she was a ghost haunting me or that I was going crazy. It wasn't until I was a teenager that I revealed these moments to my grandmother and she cried. That was the first time in my life that I witnessed my grandmother cry. I never understood why that revelation disturbed her so much. I hate to see her upset and it was worse for me if I was the source of her pain. I made a mental note to not talk about that scene with my grandmother again.

I visit my grandmother in Jamaica at least three times a year and fit the rest of my family members into my schedule throughout the year. This is the first year that I didn't have much time to spend with anyone, let alone my man. I am a few credits away from completing the Information Technology certification program, which tremendously increases my chances of launching my internet software program. Before mom's passes away she put aside a stash of money for me. Unfortunately, I can't touch that money until I am twenty-three years old. I guess she assumed at twenty-one I would be stuck on partying and at twenty-two years old, I would slowly calm down with the drinking and partying. Moms was right though. I will be twenty-three in a few months and lately drinking and partying is the last goal on my mind. When we were younger, Kimberly and I made a pact to become business owners at twenty-three years old. Kim is ahead of the game; she completed Cosmetology School and opened her Beauty Salon before she was permitted to drink alcohol legally. Kim's progression did not surprise me at all, we all know her mom, Aunt Kesha, is a go-getter and always has been. She helped me and Kim come up with our business plan way before we experienced puberty. I love Aunt Kesha's hustler mentality; it wasn't hard for me to understand why her and my mom were best friends. Although, I came from a wealthy family background, I made a lot of different decisions that changed the outcome of what life should have been for me...

ABOUT THE AUTHOR

Lady Dee was born in Fort Lauderdale, Florida. She is an entrepreneur, business woman, and writer. She writes fun, romantic, drama- filled stories that surround true events. Lady Dee knows just how to turn a seemingly ordinary love story into an unputdownable read. She also writes poetry and short stories on occasion. Her stories are told in a matter-of-fact manner, but the characters and the plot are intricate and entwined, and the premise is so original and unlike any other. Her desire is for readers to connect with the characters and take personal lessons from each story. Be prepared to have a myriad of emotions that draw you in, while reading her books!

For more information and book updates visit www.ladydeeauthor.com.